**"What could you possibly want from me?"
Trent asked.**

The unspoken words: *someone who's crippled and useless.*

"I want you to give Rana lessons."

He frowned, clearly perplexed. "Lessons?"

"She's a breakaway roper. One of the best in the county. I'd like you to help her improve."

He immediately shook his head. "Impossible. I would need to ride alongside her." He leaned forward, as if he feared she might miss his next words. "*Run* alongside her. I could barely hang on at a trot."

"Bull. You can coach her from the sidelines."

"That's a half-ass way of doing it." Sunlight hit his face head-on, illuminating his square chin and dazzling gray eyes. He sat his horse just like any other cowboy, and Alana was reminded of the cover photo she'd seen of him once upon a time in some rodeo magazine, when he'd been photographed just as he was now. Square in the saddle, one hand resting on the horn, the other holding the reins.

Handsome.

Dear Reader,

I am frequently asked where I get my ideas for books. Honestly, they come from all over the place. It's not unusual for me to be in the middle of a conversation, only to interrupt and say, "Wait! That's a great idea for a book!"

A Cowboy's Pride is an example of that happening. I was sitting at the coffee shop where I write when a friend of mine mentioned a ranch where her mother worked, a ranch that specialized in people with disabilities, a ranch in the far reaches of Northern California....

And an idea was born.

My fictional ranch is nothing like the real ranch in question, but I'd like to think the characters could be real. They certainly feel that way to me. I love a wounded hero, especially one who thinks he's unworthy of love. And I adore a heroine who's not afraid to stand up to a man, and whose heart is as big as her capacity to love.

I hope you enjoy *A Cowboy's Pride*, and that you pick up the sequel in November, if you get a chance.

Pamela

P.S. You might find it interesting to note that every horse in *A Cowboy's Pride* is an actual animal owned by either me or a friend. To see photos of the real horses, visit my Facebook page, www.facebook.com/pamelabritton.

A Cowboy's Pride

PAMELA BRITTON

HARLEQUIN® AMERICAN ROMANCE®

Recycling programs
for this product may
not exist in your area.

ISBN-13: 978-0-373-75457-1

A COWBOY'S PRIDE

Copyright © 2013 by Pamela Britton

Printed in U.S.A.

www.Harlequin.com

ABOUT THE AUTHOR

With over a million books in print, Pamela Britton likes to call herself the best-known author nobody's ever heard of. Of course, that changed thanks to a certain licensing agreement with that little racing organization known as NASCAR.

But before the glitz and glamour of NASCAR, Pamela wrote books that were frequently voted the best of the best by the *Detroit Free Press*, Barnes & Noble (two years in a row) and *RT Book Reviews*. She's won numerous awards, including a National Readers' Choice Award and a nomination for the Romance Writers of America's Golden Heart.

When not writing books, Pamela is a reporter for a local newspaper. She's also a columnist for the *American Quarter Horse Journal*.

Books by Pamela Britton

HARLEQUIN AMERICAN ROMANCE

HARLEQUIN AMERICAN ROMANCE

Larri Jo Starkey, this one's for you. I love that you read everything I write, including my adult horse stories. I love that you get my style of writing. Most of all, I feel blessed to have you as my editor at the *American Quarter Horse Journal*. Over the years you have gone from mentor to true friend. I am blessed.

Chapter One

"He's here."

Alana McClintock kept her gaze firmly on the frying pan in front of her, though she glanced up quickly at the teenager who burst into the spacious state-of-the-art kitchen like a colt from a pasture. The black cowboy hat the girl wore just about fell from her head.

"It's got to be him, Alana," the fourteen-year-old all but shouted, brown ponytail flying. "They said they'd be here around five and it's a little after that right now."

The butter-and-brown-sugar mixture began to lose its viscosity, a sure sign the homemade syrup was about to boil. "Be there in a sec."

"But you're going to miss it," the girl wailed.

There. Tiny bubbles began to form on the bottom. Alana grabbed her whisk. Timing was everything here. If she let it get too hot, it would crystallize. If she didn't get things hot enough, it would turn into a gooey mess, and Cabe and Rana wouldn't have anything to pour over their flapjacks. She'd never hear the end of it, either.

"Here comes the bus right now."

She stirred the mixture with more and more speed, then quickly counted down. Five. Four. Three. Two...

"Done." She grabbed a pot holder and clutched the cast-iron skillet, taking it off the stove. "Who needs a double boiler?"

"Hurry!"

"All right, all right."

With the pan safely off to the side and the gas off, Alana turned toward Rana. The teenager had the appearance of a kid on Christmas morning. No surprise since her hero, a man Rana had looked up to since she was old enough to watch TV and, more important, the National Finals Rodeo, was about to arrive at New Horizons Ranch.

Albeit in a wheelchair.

"Hurry," Rana cried, spinning on her heel and running from the kitchen, her cowboy boots leaving clumps of dirt on the floor.

"Rana," Alana scolded. "You know how much that drives me nuts. No boots in the house."

The teenager had disappeared.

Alana followed at a more leisurely pace. Never before had Rana shown so much enthusiasm for a guest, and there'd been a lot of guests come and go over the years. They were primarily a dude ranch, one of the best in the nation, according to a review they'd recently received, yet they did more than escort people on trail rides. They specialized in guests with disabilities. Guests who couldn't walk, guests missing limbs, guests with severe deformities. Alana provided therapy if they needed it. Sometimes it was the parents who were disabled, sometimes the children. New Horizons made sure *everyone* enjoyed the same types of activities: horseback riding, swimming and, most of all, the Feather River.

But this was the first time they'd have a single guest, and he was their first official celebrity, if people in the rodeo world could be called celebrities. Rana lived and breathed rodeo. This was her first year riding for her high school team. Her best event, breakaway roping, was similar to the kind of roping seen on TV. So when she'd heard Trent Anderson would be a guest, well, there'd been no living with the child. The world-famous All-Around Cowboy was one of Rana's all-time heroes, right behind her father, who also happened to be Alana's boss…sort of.

"Finally decided to join us," teased that boss when she stepped onto the porch a moment later. Cabe smiled, a grin so much like his brother's, Alana had to look away. Braden would have been glad to welcome Trent Anderson, too.

"You know Alana wouldn't miss this for the world." Rana clutched her dad's left hand, her gaze firmly on the bus visible through the pine trees in the front pasture. The two of them were like carbon copies of each other with their brown hair, blue eyes and small noses. They each wore blue-checkered shirts, though in different shades. Rana's was more brilliant than Cabe's, a shade of blue that matched their eyes. They both wore the same type of cowboy hat—flat—not like a John Wayne hat with a curled brim. More like Wyatt Earp's. Vaquero-style, it was called, the flat hats popular in the high desert. Rana had complemented her outfit with a butterfly-blue "wild rag," a silk bandanna that cowboys used to shield their faces from the cold. Rana had wrapped it around her neck, the ends dangling down in front of her.

"I just hope this wasn't a mistake," she heard Cabe say as she walked up next to him.

"Why would this be a mistake?" Rana tipped her head to the side to stare up at her dad.

"Usually, we've never met our guests prior to their visit."

There was something in Cabe's eyes that put Alana on alert. He was frowning as the bus approached.

"It'll be fine." Alana gently nudged his arm.

"I hope so." He gave her a smile in return.

Alana took a deep breath, filling her lungs with air that seemed scented with oregano, but was actually wild sage. They were a million miles from nowhere, in God's country, in northern California where pine trees turned the meadows army-green and snow turned the tip of an ancient volcano a glorious white. They were in a valley, one surrounded by low-lying mountains, the volcano to her northwest, though it was so far away it was difficult to gauge just how big it really was over the tops of the whispering pine trees. Just glancing at the snow made Alana pull her black thigh-length sweater tight around her. It was late afternoon, the sun hiding behind the Douglas firs so that their trunks threw long shadows onto the ground. When the light disappeared, it'd be cold.

"Why is Tom driving sooooo slow?" grumbled Rana.

She followed Rana's gaze. A yellow bus, the kind traditionally associated with schools, had turned down their driveway, the tires kicking up dust. It was almost summer, but the valley was known for its late springs, and yellow wildflowers dotted the pasture, the blooms having cropped up so quickly it was as if they celebrated the change in temperatures. Though it was California, it wasn't uncommon for frost to wreak havoc. So the wildflowers weren't the only living things to be glad the bitterly cold weather was over—Alana was grateful, too.

"Do you think he'll remember you, Dad?" Rana stood in front of her father now, her dad's arms resting upon her shoulders. She looked up and back and shot him a wide smile. He was the center of her universe. The filling in her Hostess cupcake. The espresso in her caramel macchiato. It'd been that way ever since Rana's mother died, and once again Alana had to look away as she thought back to those difficult days. So much tragedy. So much loss. And now, look. Rana had learned to walk again, and the ranch had a new name…and a new mission, and she…well, Alana had taken on the role of surrogate mother even though there was nothing romantic between her and Cabe.

"Oh, he remembers me."

Something about the way Cabe said those words had Alana glancing at him sharply. Had there been bad blood between them when Cabe had quit the rodeo circuit to nurse his little girl? Alana couldn't remember hearing anything. Of course, Cabe and Braden had competed at a different level than Trent. The brothers had just begun to take their rodeo careers seriously—flying to bigger, out-of-state rodeos, an eye on the National Finals Rodeo.

And then the car accident.

Both she and Cabe had lost loved ones. He a brother and a wife, she a future husband, and the two of them had clung to each other in their grief. There'd never been anything between them, never would be, but she'd stuck around for Rana's sake. She'd talked about moving out. Cabe and Rana wouldn't hear of it. They still needed each other, Rana said. She couldn't be without her aunt Alana. She was family, they had both insisted, the tragedy having bonded them together in a way none of them could have imagined. In fact, the similarities between what had happened to them and what had happened to their new guest, Trent, gave Alana chills.

Could they fix him like they'd fixed Rana?

Something hissed. Alana jerked back only to realize the bus had pulled to a stop in front of the old farmhouse that had been in Trent's family for decades—a massive three-story straight-up-and-down affair with old-fashioned sash windows and a jagged roofline meant to ward off snow. They'd built her a small single-story apartment opposite the massive lawn that stretched across the backyard. It was cozy, but comfy, and exclusively hers.

"Here we go," Cabe said as the door folded open.

She leaned forward. He was the only guest arriving today. With the whir and whine of an electric motor, a ramp unfolded, and Alana caught her first glimpse of the rodeo hero inside, although she couldn't see much. He sat slumped in his wheelchair, face in profile, the only thing that stood out clearly his off-white cowboy hat.

"Welcome to the New Horizons Ranch," Rana pronounced, tipping up on her toes in excitement.

No response.

By now, Alana's eyes had adjusted. What she saw was a chiseled profile instantly recognizable as the one from TV. A chin so square it would do Dudley Do-Right proud, although not in a bad way. He was handsome. She had once heard someone refer to him as "hot," thanks to his tanned skin, silver-buckle-colored eyes and dark blond hair. He had wide shoulders—not that you could see that now, not with him slumped over as he was. It looked as though he hadn't shaved in a few days, his jaw and chin covered by at least a week's worth of stubble. The button-down white shirt he wore under his jacket even looked rumpled.

"Good to see you, Trent," Cabe called out.

No response.

Tom hopped inside, pressed the button that Alana knew would release the chair. With the ease of someone who'd done the same thing a million times, the driver spun the seat around toward them, the longtime rodeo hero suddenly face-to-face with the small crowd that had gathered to greet him.

"Welcome to New Horizons Ranch," Rana repeated happily.

Still no response.

"Long time no see," Cabe added softly.

The cowboy didn't look at them. Didn't so much as lift his head. Not a muscle twitched.

Tom pushed the wheelchair onto the lift. Sunlight illuminated Trent Anderson's form. Still the same broad shoulders. The same narrow midsection. He wore a denim jacket over the white shirt and matching denim jeans, looking for all the world like the Trent from TV. It was the legs that looked different. They hung limply in front of him. And, of course, there was no horse.

"Don't expect much of a conversation from him," said Tom. "He hasn't said two words since I fetched him from the airport. Starting to think he lost his voice along with the use of his legs."

That got a reaction.

"I can still walk," Trent muttered.

Barely, from what she'd heard. Rana had filled her in based on internet accounts. Partial paralysis of both legs from midthigh down. He'd hurt his back. There'd been talk he'd never walk again. Or ride. The fact that he had some feeling in his upper legs was a miracle, she'd been told.

"I'll show you to your cabin, Mr. Anderson," Rana said, coming forward to take over for the driver.

"Don't touch me."

Both Tom and Rana leaned back.

"I can do it myself." His hands grabbed the wheels, spinning the aluminum frame expertly around.

Alana took one look at Rana's crushed face and jumped in front of the man.

"*You* have no idea where you're going." She placed her hands on her hips and dared him to try to run her down.

"I'll find my way."

He swerved around her. She jumped ahead again.

"You'll stay right here while we fetch your bags."

For the first time, steel-gray eyes met her own. "There's only one. Put it in my lap."

Put it in my lap.

As if she was some kind of lackey or something.

She met Cabe's gaze, then looked over at the bus driver. They both stared at her with a mix of surprise and dismay. Tom held a small black duffel bag. She motioned for him to toss it in her direction, and when he did, immediately rebounded it into the cowboy's lap.

"First cabin on the left." She stepped to the side. "Don't let the front door hit you in the ass."

Three stunned faces gazed back at her, though she didn't bother looking at Trent again. Yeah, she might have sounded harsh, but something about the man instantly drove her nuts.

Jerk.

Too bad she would have to put up with him for three weeks.

She heard him set off, the wheels of his chair crunching on the gravel. Using the main road, it was a long, long way to the cabins, through the parklike area that surrounded the old ranch house, down past the trees where they thickened up, then down a small hill to the left where the road opened up and the cabins sat—eight of them—the lodge-pine dwellings to the left and the Feather River to the right. That was why Rana had offered to show him the way. Using the road, one part was pretty steep. Sure, she'd probably hoped to talk to him about roping, too. Guess that wasn't going to happen. With any luck maybe he'd make a wrong turn and end up on somebody else's property.

Now, now, Alana. You need to be nice. Obviously, the guy has issues.

Yeah, and those issues were now their problem. Great.

"Thanks for bringing him out here," she said to Tom, her mock smile indicating she felt anything but gratitude.

She turned back to Trent. "Hey," she called out to the cowboy who, surprisingly enough, stopped, though he didn't look back. "Welcome to New Horizons Ranch."

She saw his fists clench and would bet her favorite bay gelding that he did so to keep from flipping her off.

She smiled.

He turned back just in time to catch it.

"Thanks" was all he said before setting off again.

"He's never going to make it all the way down there without some help," she heard Rana mutter.

"I know," Alana said.

"He probably thinks the guest quarters are nearby," the girl added.

"He'll learn otherwise soon enough," Alana muttered.

"Should I tell him about the footpath behind the barn?" Rana asked. "That's a much safer route for someone in a wheelchair."

Alana glanced at Cabe, and when she saw the small smile alight upon his face, said, "I think we'll let him figure things out on his own."

So it was that all three of them watched as the stubborn man moved farther and farther down the road, completely oblivious to the fact that there was a special trail for people with disabilities. But Alana figured if she mentioned the trail she'd probably upset him even more. She could tell he was the type of man who didn't like the "disabled" label at all.

"You think he'll stay the whole three weeks?" Rana asked,

and Alana noticed she had tears in her eyes. Poor girl's feelings were hurt.

Alana heard Cabe huff. "I think we'll be lucky if he lasts three days."

Alana gave him twenty-four hours.

Chapter Two

Welcome to New Horizons Ranch.

Trent jerked the chair forward with a thrust of his hand, knowing he hadn't been exactly friendly to Cabe's girlfriend, but little caring.

He didn't want to be here.

Cabe had to know that. The man had been part of the scheme to get him to New Horizons Ranch, along with Trent's mom and his best friend, Saedra.

It's time to get your life back on track. Time to rejoin the land of the living. New Horizons Ranch will help you do that.

His mom was dead wrong.

Being a "guest" at a ranch owned by some guy he barely knew wasn't going to accomplish anything. Scratch that. It would accomplish one thing. He'd end up humiliating himself in front of Cabe and that pretty little friend of his, never mind his daughter. The girl would get over the hero worship once she realized his glory days were over.

His stomach twisted.

He thrust down on his wheels harder, enjoying the exercise, not caring that the sweat beaded up on his brow. Pine trees dotted the roadside, the long trunks thin in some spots, thick in others. He'd glimpsed a riding arena and a barn back there, to the left of the road.

Where the hell were those cabins?

He paused for a moment, huffing as he looked around.

Had he missed a turnoff? He was far enough away from the old ranch house now that he couldn't see it. A grove of thick trees blocked his view.

Should he go back?

"Need some help?"

Son of a—

"I'm fine," he said, pushing off again.

"You don't know where you're going," she called out after him.

"Obviously I can't be too far away if you're here." He glanced back at her, observing that black tail of hair so thick it reminded him of a draft horse's, which might not be very flattering, but the damn stuff was a thick mass. "What'd you do? Cut through the trees?"

And those eyes. Such a light blue he found himself wanting to look back just to get another peek at them. Instead he pushed on. Obviously, he hadn't missed a road.

"Shortcut," she called out after him. "Makes it easier to get to our guests."

Damn it. He hated gravel roads. And dirt roads. The wheels of the chair would hook on a rock and pitch to the right or left. He constantly had to correct himself.

"Though I'm curious what you're going to do when you reach the hill."

He hands paused, but only for a second. "I'll be fine."

"We usually escort our guests to their cabins," she added. "You know…for safety reasons."

His hands would work as brakes.

"Or we have Tom drop them off."

Whatever.

"We've only had one person attempt that hill in a wheelchair all by themselves. You should have seen it. Reminded me of sled racing in the Olympics—"

"Okay, fine." He spun his chair to face her, nearly pitching his bag off his lap in the process. "You can help me down there, though I don't know why Cabe sent his girlfriend along to do his dirty work."

"I'm not his girlfriend."

She wasn't?

"And he sent me because he's busy dealing with his daughter, who's a tad upset right now because a man she's worshipped for years just snapped at her."

He looked into her eyes then, spotted the disappointment and disgust and, yes, the loathing that she felt for him.

"So I offered to come and help you out, although I was tempted to let you navigate that hill all on your own. With any luck you'd have kept right on going and landed in the river, maybe even been carried downstream where you'd become someone else's problem."

She really didn't like him. If he were honest with himself, he didn't blame her. He didn't like himself much these days, either.

"I don't want to be here," he heard himself admit. Funny, he'd promised himself he'd stick it out—if only for his mom's sake—and yet here he was confessing the truth to a woman he'd just met.

She had the dignity to soften her gaze. "A lot of people are afraid to come here, at least at first. They worry they won't be able to enjoy themselves. Or that the therapy portion of their days will hurt. Or that their families will enjoy themselves and they won't. But you know what? At least those people aren't afraid to confront a challenge head-on."

Ouch.

She meant the words as an insult, and it worked. That stung him right in his belly.

"Some people come here for their families, for a chance to do something with the people they love for the first time in years. But I don't think I've ever met someone so instantly hostile as you are, so if you're going to continue to be an ass, I might as well push you back to the main house. It's not too late to call Tom and have him take you back to the airport."

Was that a challenge she'd just issued?

"What's it going to be, cowboy?" She stared him down like a wild horse in a rodeo, daring a cowboy to stay on.

He tipped his chin up. "I've never backed away from anything in my life."

He saw her eyes narrow, saw that gaze flicker over him as if doubtful he would amount to anything, the expression in her eyes setting his temper to flare in a way he hadn't felt in, well, in a long, long while.

"We'll see."

Alana insisted on following him, even though he made it clear he didn't want her to. He didn't want her to help him, either, but when he saw the size of the hill leading into the river valley, he changed his mind. Alana almost laughed at the way he grudgingly allowed her to guide his chair.

"We're pretty secluded out here." She motioned to the log cabin where he'd be residing, the sun's rays catching the color of the wood and turning it gold. They were making their way toward a low-lying valley, one with a wide swath of lawn to the left with pine trees sprouting up at odd intervals. They'd had cabins built among the trees, the resulting vista something Alana was proud of having had a hand in. Across from the cabins was the Feather River, and though winter was gone, the water still rushed past with a gentle roar thanks to the snowpack in the hills.

"There are landline phones in every room if you ever need any help." She leaned back, trying to counterbalance the weight of him in his chair with her own. Too bad they hadn't had Tom take him down. That would have made things easier. Then again, if they'd done that, she wouldn't be able to give him such a hard time. And if ever a man needed a hard time, this man did.

"I won't need help."

Hah.

But the words confirmed her suspicion that it really got under his skin when she reminded him of the *disabled* word.

So she resolved to use it as much as possible.

She patted him on the shoulder patronizingly. "We're here for you, Trent. We specialize in helping disabled guests."

They were halfway down the hill, and she would bet if he didn't fear a runaway wheelchair, he would have used his hands to jerk away from her.

"Once I get to my cabin, I want to be left alone."

He sounded like a petulant child, and in a way he was. He was having to learn how to walk again, was completely dependent on other people to teach him to do exactly that. Things he'd taken for granted were no longer easy—like making his way to a cabin in the woods. And as she thought about all that he'd had to overcome, including the death of his best friends in the tragic car wreck that had almost cost him his life, well, suffice it to say she started to wonder if she wasn't being a little too hard on him.

That was until they reached the bottom of the hill and he did exactly what she knew he'd been dying to do. He wrenched away.

"Damn." She stopped and rested her hands on her hips, her fingers stinging from the force of the handles being ripped from her grasp. "You're good at that."

He ignored her, just made a beeline for his cabin. He must have seen that it was handicapped equipped because he zipped toward the place as if he rode in a two-wheeled sports car. A ramp had been built to run straight up to the front door. His wheels hit the slats with a clackity-click-click. His bag nearly slipped from his lap he stopped so hard as he spun his chair so he could push on the handle.

"It's locked," she called out in a singsong voice, knowing it wasn't very nice of her to take such naughty pleasure in his impatience.

He glanced at the door, then her, clearly frustrated.

She contemplated for an instant how it would feel to walk away and leave him there. She wished she had the gumption to do exactly that, but in the end, she really did understand what he was going through. She'd watched Rana go through the same type of emotional turmoil. Grief was tricky. It brought out either the best or the worst in people. If he was anything like her, he felt the loss of his friend like a kick to the stomach.

She headed for the front door.

Sunlight turned the surface of the wood-framed window into a mirror. She spotted her reflection as she walked toward the cabin. Reflected, too, was the image of blue sky, the mercury-like surface of the river and the meadow that lined the water's edge, and the low-lying mountains.

"Here." She turned the key with a flourish. The smell of pine and beeswax greeted her as she opened the door. "Light switch to the right. Bathroom straight ahead, just before the bedroom. It's handicapped equipped, by the way."

He rolled past her. She caught the scent of him then, an interesting combination of citrus and cinnamon, which she might have taken a moment to admire if he wasn't a guest and a soon-to-be patient. He really was good with that chair, judging by the way he wheeled around the small table and chairs to their right. He paused in the sitting room area that lined the front of the cabin. To her surprise he suddenly faced her, cowboy hat momentarily shielding his gaze until he lifted his chin.

"Tell the girl I'm sorry."

It took a moment to realize who he was talking about.

The hat dipped down again. She saw his jaw work, the little muscle along the side of it ticking as if he were grinding his teeth.

"Long flight."

He leaned forward, suddenly slipping out of the jacket he wore and exposing a toned upper body covered by a white button-down shirt.

My, my, my.

As patients went, he was pretty dang easy on the eyes.

"Three-hour flight from Colorado to the West Coast, another wait to catch the small plane that brought me here, then a long drive to what felt like the middle of nowhere, all to get to a place I don't want to be."

Maybe he wasn't such an ass after all.

She studied him anew. He really was a handsome cuss with his dented chin and his piercing gray eyes. She could see why girls the world over had followed his rodeo career.

"You really should give the place a try." She clutched her sweater around her tighter. Good-looking or not, this man came with a lot of baggage. "It's worked wonders for some people."

His chin moved up a notch. "You some kind of therapist or something?"

She almost laughed. "Didn't you know?"

"Know what?"

"That's what I do here. Physical therapy. And cook on occasion for Cabe and Rana, although Cabe's the better cook. I do make a mean pot of chili, though."

He stared at her anew, looked at her hard. She could see the wheels turning behind those pretty eyes of his.

"You were Braden Jensen's fiancée, weren't you?"

The nerves of her face suddenly turned cold.

"I remember seeing you at the Pendleton show. He told me you were in college. That you were studying sports medicine. That you wanted to help athletes with injuries."

Breathe, Alana. Breathe.

"We weren't officially engaged," she heard herself say. "He hadn't asked me yet, but we'd talked about it. After…*it* happened, I learned he'd bought me a ring. He was going to ask me at Christmas."

And that had been a lifetime ago.

His gaze flicked over her, as if assessing her for damage, too. When their eyes locked again, there was an expression in his, one that made her face come back to life, her skin blazing with color.

Get the hell out of here, Alana.

"Dial zero if you need to reach the main house." She crossed her arms in front of herself, for some reason uncomfortable with this new and more friendly version of Trent Anderson.

"Breakfast will be brought to you around eight, unless you think you're capable of making your own."

"I can take care of myself."

"Good. Your refrigerator is fully stocked. We have a cleaning service that comes in once a day. Just hang out the sign on the door if you'd rather we leave things alone."

"Is that why you stick around? Is this *your* therapy?"

Go to hell.

"I'll see you tomorrow, Mr. Anderson."

Because, no, this wasn't her therapy. She was here for Rana, a girl who needed her mother, but who'd lost her instead. She might be a poor substitute, but she loved Rana like a daughter. The therapy? That was just a job, a good job, one she enjoyed. Helping people was her calling in life, always had been. Of course, she'd assumed she'd use her degree working for the Professional Bull Rider's Association or something. How ironic that she might find herself treating the very type of athlete she'd originally trained to help.

"I guess I'm not the only one with old wounds," she heard him call out.

"Good night, Mr. Anderson."

Ignore him.

She *was* over Braden. She had been for years.

At least, that's what she told herself.

Chapter Three

She dreaded the coming day.

The moment her eyes popped open, Alana groaned.

Trent Anderson.

The good-looking son of a gun was going to be a royal pain in her behind. She could tell. Normally, that wouldn't pose much of a problem. She'd dealt with her share of unpleasant clients over the years. They were rare. As she'd told Trent, most people came to New Horizons Ranch of their own free will, but every once in a while someone would come along who would try her patience.

Yeah, but they weren't good-looking...like Trent.

She shoved her pillow over her head and groaned. And, okay, she could admit to herself that over the years when she'd spotted Trent on TV once or twice, maybe she might have noted to herself that he was a good-looking man. With his cocky cowboy attitude, he was the kind of guy most women drooled over—herself included—although never in an ooh-I-wish-I-could-date-him kind of way. Nope. Never.

She whipped the covers off, determined to begin her day even though a part of her wanted to stay in bed with the covers firmly over her head.

A half hour later she stepped onto the tiny porch built off her home. The little house was blue with picture windows and trim that matched the main homestead. Cabe and Rana had wanted her to stay with them, but tongues had started to wag in town over their sleeping arrangements, especially after a year had passed, so Cabe had built her the cabin. It was perfect.

"Brrr."

Chilly. Go figure. The black poufy jacket did little to keep her warm this time of morning. That was the problem with living at a higher elevation, she thought, stepping onto the gravel path that led to the barn. Nights and mornings were always cold, thanks to a snow-cooled breeze that blew in from the mountains. One learned to dress in layers, because by noon it'd be warm again. But nothing could beat the view, she admitted, passing beneath a thick stand of pine trees that surrounded Cabe's backyard. Gray mountains in the distance. Meadows nearby. And a sky so blue it looked almost purple. Paradise.

Her breath misted as she stepped beneath the trees' canopy. Soon enough, she spotted the arena. To her left was the barn, a state-of-the-art facility with room for twelve horses, an office above that featured windows across the front and side, and a board-and-batten exterior painted white. It looked as though the barn was made out of wood, but it was really made out of an artificial compound resistant to fire, not that you'd ever guess.

It looked so pretty sitting there this early in the morning, diffused sunlight painting the outside a pale orange, steam rising off the dark green roof above. The weather vane pointed west, she noticed. That was why it was so cold. Wind coming in from the hills, just as she'd suspected.

A horse spotted her. Its neigh echoed across the stable yard between the barn and the arena.

"I'm coming, I'm coming."

Behind the barn was the main pasture, the ranch horses that they used for guests grazing in the distance, and behind them a faint line of trees that signaled the Bureau of Land Management's property line. Cabe had the grazing rights.

A horse nickered impatiently, its knee bumping the stall door. "All right," Alana said, less patiently. She turned toward an open area to her left filled to the brim with grass hay. "Sheesh, you guys."

It wasn't her job to feed the horses, not really. Cabe usually took care of it, but when she was up early enough and she had no guests to attend, she didn't mind lending a hand. She enjoyed feeding the horses, loved the smell of a freshly opened bale of hay. Alana inhaled deeply as she grabbed a flake, then turned around. She couldn't help but smile at the horses' looks of anticipation.

"Hey," Cabe said from her right. Alana paused, a flake of oat hay in hand, the rich, loamy scent filling her nose. The horse she'd been about to feed stamped its foot in impatience, sending up a flurry of dust that caught the early morning light, particles swirling through the air.

"What are you doing up so early?"

Gray eyes and dark blond hair flashed into her mind.

"Couldn't sleep," she said. Trent's handsome face had haunted her all dang night.

"Oh?" Cabe teased as he walked toward her. "Guess he really got under your skin, too, huh?"

It bugged the you-know-what out of her that Cabe could read her so easily. She thought about denying it, but she knew better than to try to con her best and oldest friend, so she frowned, shaking her head a bit.

"I have a feeling he's going to be a real pain in the rear." She tossed the flake of hay through the feed door, much to the bay gelding's delight.

"He'll settle in."

He'd stopped in front of her—Cabe Jensen, one hundred percent cowboy in his dusty brown Carhartt overalls, with a dark green button-down shirt beneath.

"You make him sound like a new horse."

Cabe pressed his lips together, considering her words, then moved to the edge of the stall so he could peer through the metal bars that kept the horses' heads away from guests, his gaze sweeping over the animal she'd just fed. Jacob. His best rope horse.

"He might be as fractious as a new horse." He met her gaze,

obviously satisfied with what he saw. Cabe wore the same cowboy hat he'd worn for years, one that was black but looked faded these days, its flat brim warped and somewhat frayed.

"Just remember—" he tucked his hands in his pockets—probably because they were cold "—it wasn't long ago that we were dealing with similar emotions from Rana."

It was true, and something she'd reminded herself of at least a hundred times last night. Somehow, though, it was different coming from Cabe. Trent wasn't family, and his good looks made her uncomfortable. There. She could admit that.

"I just hope he'll at least try some of the therapies I suggest. I'm not even certain he'll let me assess the damage done to his legs."

"Maybe you can do that without actually examining him."

"How?"

Cabe smirked. "I was giving it some thought last night and I agree. He doesn't want to be here, but to be honest, I was already warned about that. So I was thinking we need to outsmart him."

"You were warned?"

A crafty look entered Cabe's eyes. "I called his mom last night. She told me it took all her persuasive powers to get Trent on the plane. Apparently, he called her last night, too, and he made it perfectly clear he wasn't happy."

"Oh, great." She could understand reluctance, but out-and-out hostility would make things difficult.

"That's what I'm saying. We need to outsmart him."

"And how do you propose we do that?"

"Put him up on a horse today."

She lost her power of speech for a moment. Well, that wasn't exactly true. A million things bubbled through her mind, but she couldn't voice them…except for her next words. "You're kidding, right?"

"Why not? He has partial use of his upper legs. He should be able to hold on just fine."

"Yeah, if he had some training."

"That's what the special saddle we use is for. He won't fall off."

"You're right, he won't because he's not going to agree to it."

Amusement filled his face, wrinkles crinkling the corners of his mouth all the way to the line of his jaw. "Doesn't hurt to ask."

Her boss had lost his mind.

The words repeated themselves as she went about her morning chores. Truth was, she was a lot more than a therapist. She wore a lot of hats: cook, chauffer, ranch hand. No two days were ever alike, so as they headed into breakfast it didn't take her by surprise when Cabe said, "You going to check on him this morning, or shall I?"

The words *you do it* almost escaped her lips. One thing stopped her—the twinkle in Cabe's eyes. It was as if he dared her to beard the lion in his den, and to be honest, Alana wasn't as averse to the idea as he might think. It wouldn't hurt to show the man that she wasn't intimidated.

"I'll do it."

An hour later she brought the John Deere Mule—an ATV-like vehicle with a miniature truck cabin and bed—to a coasting stop in front of Trent's temporary home, the tires crunching on the drive. There was no reason to have butterflies in her stomach, she told herself. He might be a rodeo legend, but his injuries were all the proof she should need that he was also just a man.

"Knock, knock," she said, rapping lightly on the door.

Of course, there was always the chance he wasn't up yet. She'd no sooner had the thought than she caught a whiff of maple-cured bacon, the sweet smell making her stomach growl. They'd had oatmeal for breakfast. Boring.

"Hello?"

Would he ignore her? She had to admit, it was totally possible. He might choose to stay in his cabin the whole—

The door opened.

Good Lord, he wasn't dressed.

Her mouth dropped open next.

"Yes?"

Keep your eyes up.

But it was hard when he had an upper body that would rival an action figure—six rippling, symmetrical bulges that decreased in size the lower her gaze drifted, and it drifted lower. His skin was a soft gold in color—and damn it, her eyes kept traveling lower and lower despite her best efforts, her cheeks turning molten when she spotted the tiny wisps of brown hair that seemed to point toward—

"I, um…"

Pull it together, Alana.

His gray eyes. *Focus on those.* "I was, um, asked to check on you."

Not check him out, Alana!

"I'm fine."

Yes, you certainly are.

She coughed, sputtered, tried gasping in a breath. What was with her? She was acting like a sex-starved adolescent.

Yes, and when, exactly, was the last time you had sex?

"Are you okay?"

"Fine," she wheezed, her mind mentally scooting away from the question. "Did you need anything?"

Coffee? Tea? *Me?*

She almost—*almost*—laughed.

"I've been able to take care of myself for months."

"I see."

He stared up at her. She stared down at him. He smirked.

She snapped, "Cabe wants us all to go on a ride today."

His turn to be caught off guard. "Excuse me?"

"Cabe. He said—"

"I heard you, but I won't be going." He jerked his hands on his wheels, rolling back like a race car driver. His hand found the door.

"Whoa, there, ace." She shoved her foot in so fast, she bit

back a gasp of pain when it slammed into her. "That wasn't a request."

If a look could incinerate a person, she should have been a puff of smoke. Or maybe a black smudge on the ground.

"I'm in no condition to ride."

She smiled brightly. "Someone will be down to pick you up at ten in the morning." She gave him her sweetest I-don't-care-what-you-think smile. "I'll see you then."

Two HOURS LATER they were all standing outside the barn. Alana had just finished saddling up her horse, and she played with the dark bay's forelock. Cabe was to her left, saddling up one of two horses—a bay and a gray—that he had tied to the hitching post to the right of the barn. Opposite the hitching post stood what looked like parallel bars, a deck built next to them and a handicap ramp that led to the top. They'd have to use that if Trent actually agreed to Cabe's crazy idea. Not that he would agree. Too bad, too, because it really might be good for him.

She soothed her horse's forelock down.

You're fussing.

No, she wasn't.

Nerves.

It wasn't that, she firmly told herself. Trent Anderson didn't make her nervous.

Yeah, right.

"Go on down and get him," Cabe said as he tightened the cinch on a big bay-colored horse wearing a saddle that looked like a cross between a barber's chair and a car seat. A specialty saddle, it was called. This one had a seat back that was shoulder high and a wide leather strap where a man's waist would be. "I'll be done here in a sec."

The animal pinned its ears and wrinkled its nose in protest when Cabe tugged on the leather strap. "Uh-uh," he warned. "Enough of that. Only one cranky male allowed on the ranch."

And that would be Trent.

"You want *me* to go get him?" The last thing she wanted was to deal with Trent Anderson. "Rana should do it." She glanced past the rump of her horse.

Rana, who was busy feeding a carrot to Ellie, turned sharply when she heard the words. She'd been the first one to finish saddling up her sorrel mare. "I don't think so."

She'd been kidding…sort of. After yesterday's disastrous first meeting, she wasn't about to send the teenager to deal with the surly cowboy.

"I don't blame you," Alana grumbled.

"I'm sending you because you're a good-looking woman he won't say no to." Cabe gave her a wicked grin, one meant to tease the irritation off her face. It didn't work.

"I think we should all ride the horses down together. You know, shame the jerk into doing it. We can lead Baylor down there with us."

"That won't be necessary."

Alana groaned. She knew who stood in the barn aisle to her right, didn't need to glance behind her to verify it. So she didn't. The damn man must have found the hiking path they'd constructed for people in wheelchairs, the same path he could have taken yesterday—if he'd been civil.

She pushed away from the hitching post, checked her horse's girth, pasted a huge smile on her face, then turned and said, "Glad to see you found the trail." Not that it would have been hard to spot. There were signs pointing to it all over the ranch.

He ignored her comment. "I came up here to tell you I'm not going."

Big surprise.

"You *are* going," she said, "even if I have to be the one to hoist you up on your horse."

She moved around the rear of Radical, her own dark bay mount, meeting the man's gaze for the first time.

He was livid.

And just as handsome as he had been this morning, darn it all to hell, but at least he'd put his dang shirt on. Still, the white button-down did little to conceal his muscular frame.

She'd been hoping the butterflies in her stomach had been a reaction to seeing a half-naked man…since she hadn't seen a half-naked male in, well, a long time. But, no. That wasn't it at all because, as she stared into those silver-gray eyes beneath the off-white cowboy hat, she became acutely aware of how gangly she'd always felt, and of how dowdy she must look with her hair all loose, her light blue shirt tucked into the waist of her jeans and stall dust all over her face. She fidgeted with her horse's forelock again.

Stop it.

"The only way you'll get me up on that horse is if you knock me senseless."

"That can be arranged," she muttered.

Cabe stepped in between them. "Trent, your mom told me to tell you to do as you're told."

Trent tipped his head back, glaring from beneath the brim of his hat. "I'm not ten years old."

"No, but I was told to tell you Anderson men don't shy away from anything. And that if your dad were alive, he'd be ashamed of your lack of 'try.'"

Alana turned in time to watch the words change the landscape of Trent's face. His eyes narrowed. His mouth pinched together. His cheeks filled with color. Brows that matched his dark blond hair came together in a frown. He hooked her with his gaze, the depth of his emotions bringing back memories of her own horrible loss, and Cabe's and Rana's, too.

"Fine."

No, a little voice told her. It would never be fine. Not for him. Nothing would ever be the same again—and she knew exactly how that felt. A surge of sympathy rolled through her.

But it was more than that.

It would never be fine between the two of them, either, because no matter how hard she tried, she couldn't stop the attraction that tickled her insides.

And that worried her most of all.

Chapter Four

He wanted to kill his mother.

Anderson men don't shy away from anything.

Yeah, well, none of the Anderson men had ever been paralyzed from the waist down. Okay, okay...not entirely paralyzed. He still had partial feeling in his thighs. And some feeling in his lower extremities, too, but it was spotty at best, and it had spelled the end of his rodeo career.

Still, though he tried to banish the words, he found himself wondering how many times he'd heard them over the years. First when he was little and in the mutton-busting events, then later when he'd decided to try bull riding. He closed his eyes, his hands aching he held them so tightly clenched. Back then, he'd been scared. Hell, if you weren't scared of riding a bull, you had no business riding them. His father used to tell him that, too.

When he opened his eyes, his mouth tightened into a mirthless smile.

And the bitch of it, the thing that should make him laugh right now, was that he hadn't been maimed by a bull. No. He'd been ruined by a worthless piece of shit with four DUIs. A man who'd been so drunk, he'd walked away from the wreck without a scratch on him while he'd barely escaped with his life, and Dustin...

He closed his eyes again. Dear God, he didn't want to think about Dustin.

"We have a mounting block for people with disabilities over there."

His eyes sprang open. Alana stared down at him...and was it his imagination? Or had that pretty blue gaze softened? She caught a glimpse of his hands again, and Trent unclenched them instantly. The only limbs that still functioned without a problem: his hands and arms.

"I can help you mount," she added. And, yes, her eyes had definitely lost their edge.

"I can do it myself." He gritted his teeth.

"Okay." She stepped back.

He jammed his cowboy hat down on his head in determination. But as he turned toward the ramp, he almost balked when he caught sight of the saddle again. It was ridiculous. Like a bar stool built into the back of a horse. It was even padded with red leather like a stupid stool.

He pushed his chair forward. What would they do? Strap him in as if he was some kind of felon?

Every inch he traveled, every second that passed, his wheels turned slower and slower until, at long last, he stopped at the base of the ramp, staring at the horse with mutiny in his heart.

"Are you sure you don't want some help?" he heard the teenager ask. He bit back an immediate retort, words that he knew would be colored by irritation.

"No."

The ramp didn't concern him. It was getting on the horse. He'd be damned if he asked for any help, not with *that woman* watching his every move. Cabe had led the bay gelding between some parallel bars with a platform built up next to them, the bars holding the animal in place.

For special-needs people...*like him.*

The sickness returned, the same woozy feeling he'd gotten when he'd woken up in the hospital and tried to slip from the bed...only to find he couldn't move his legs.

Anderson men don't shy away from anything.

His chest expanded as he took increasingly deeper and

deeper breaths. The ramp was grooved to allow for tire traction, and at such a gentle incline he doubted anyone would have issues. Still, he felt the muscles tighten in his arms, felt his breath begin to labor as he shoved his wheels forward. His heart pounded. His mouth had gone dry, too, but damned if he let *that woman* see how he struggled.

He made it to the top in seconds, expertly spinning his chair to face the horse and the ridiculous saddle. The deck was at the perfect level, the saddle sitting waist high. It should be a simple matter to pull up alongside the animal then lift himself on the horse's back, just like he did getting into a chair.

Then why did it seem as if he were about to lift weights, his breath whistling past his lips, every muscle in his shoulders strung as tight as a guide wire?

Just lift and swing.

Onto a horse!

A terrified yell, that's what the words sounded like in his skull, a litany of other words pounding between his ears.

You haven't been on a horse since the accident. No horse is completely trustworthy. What if it moves? What if you fall?

This is a bad *idea.*

But he would not, under any circumstances, back away from the challenge his mother's words had evoked. And so he rolled his chair as close to the saddle as he could, glancing at the bay gelding. The horse didn't look one iota interested. In fact, it had its head down, its lower lip hanging…as if it were asleep.

See that, Trent, they put you on the old nag. A horse you wouldn't be caught dead riding a year ago.

He trembled, yes, trembled in anger at the whole situation, at his life, at the fact he felt goaded into doing this, that he was even here, at this ranch, when all he wanted to do was be back home in Colorado. Still, he reached for the saddle, slowly testing his weight on the padded seat as he prepared to slip from his chair to the horse's back.

The horse didn't move.

Quickly, before he could think better of it, he shifted from his wheelchair to the saddle, sitting sideways for a moment before using his hands to lift his right leg and somehow managing to get it swung over the saddle's horn, the limb, like his left leg, dropping like an anchor.

"Good job," the girl cried.

He was on a horse, could actually feel the saddle beneath his butt. He tried clenching his thighs, but he only had marginal feeling in them. Still, it might be enough to hold on…if he clenched hard enough.

"Well done," Cabe echoed.

On a horse for the first time in almost a year. On a horse that hadn't moved an inch and that seemed to realize he was a damn useless human being. His breath hitched as he inhaled, his eyes suddenly burning hot.

Don't you dare blubber.

He closed his eyes, waited a few breaths, then opened them again.

He wasn't useless. He would find something to do. Anything had to be better than staring at four walls.

Feeling sorry for yourself.

When he opened his eyes again, Cabe was staring up at him, but another person was by his side. Alana stood there, too, and she was smiling, her own eyes rimmed with tears.

"Congratulations," she said softly. "You're back on."

If she'd been hoping to lift his spirits, her words had the opposite effect. "I might be back on, but I still can't ride."

His words came out like a death ray, melting her pretty little smile.

"Not yet." She glanced at Cabe. "Not yet." She appeared to take a deep breath. "We usually walk on either side of our guests when they ride for the first time. Did you need us to do that?"

Like he was some kind of toddler on a pony ride? "No."

"I didn't think you would."

Alana mounted her own horse less than ten minutes later, but you'd have thought they had just secured Trent Anderson to a medieval torture device, so loudly did he protest. The man still grumbled under his breath.

"Okay, let's go," Cabe said, swinging up onto his own horse.

"This is ridiculous," she heard Trent say. "I can hold on. You didn't need to strap me into this thing."

She risked glancing in his direction, although she sensed if he caught her staring, he wouldn't be pleased. The man seemed to have taken an instant dislike to her. Well, the feeling was mutual, never mind how good-looking he was.

"It's for your own safety," Rana said. "Even though you might feel capable of balancing in the saddle, we can't risk you falling off, especially since you don't want us to spot you while you're riding." She grinned at him. "Try and use your leg to kick Baylor forward."

"I'm a paraplegic," Trent shouted right back. "How the hell am I supposed to do that?"

To give Rana credit, she didn't let his words faze her. "You're a partial paraplegic."

Alana almost smiled. The girl sounded forty, not fourteen.

"Your horse responds to hip movement," Rana added. "A portion of your thighs still work, so use them. Pretend you're kicking. It'll move your hips, which will cue Baylor forward."

"No, it won't."

"Yes, it will. I know. I was once a paraplegic, too, a full paraplegic, so don't tell me what you can and cannot do."

Way to go, Rana, Alana thought. *Don't let him push you around.* She shifted her gaze to Trent. The look on his face was priceless.

"You had a spinal injury?" he asked.

Cabe kicked his horse forward then. "Didn't you know? That's how we got into this gig."

No, he hadn't been told. Alana could see that. So what was he guy doing here? From what Cabe had told her, this was supposedly some kind of last resort, but he clearly didn't want anything to do with therapy.

It was her turn to nudge her horse forward. "It's time you

rejoined the land of the living, Trent." She met his gaze head on. "So either kick that horse forward, or get left behind."

She gave Cabe and Rana a look, one that clearly said to follow her lead. They did.

"Hey," she heard Trent call out.

Rana went so far as to kick her horse into a lope, Cabe following suit. Alana didn't glance back.

"Hey!"

Keep riding, Alana.

"Don't you dare leave me here."

Reluctantly, she pulled on the reins, but only because she'd caught the edge of panic to his voice. But when she turned back, the man wasn't even looking at her. Rage had him contorting atop that horse like a Jedi Knight trying to use the force. Alana almost laughed, although there was nothing funny about the situation.

"Use your hips," she called out.

He could move them. Patients with an L2-S5 injury had movement through the pelvis. Some even had moderate to mild use of their limbs below the waist—like Trent. But the man acted as if he were a quadriplegic.

"Try pretending you're scooting a chair forward."

Miracle of miracles, the man finally listened, his hips thrusting so forcefully, it was a good thing they'd strapped him in. He'd have toppled forward otherwise.

The horse moved.

"There you go."

He did it again. Baylor took another step. Alana turned her horse toward the pasture.

But when she caught up with everyone at the pasture gate, Alana turned back in time to watch Trent thrust his hips forward like he had a hula hoop around his legs and not a horse between them. Baylor ambled along, the animal's head low to the ground, legs slowly moving in tune with Trent's hips.

"Good thing we didn't just rob a bank," Alana quipped.

Cabe smiled at her. "You know, you were pretty hard on the man."

She slouched in the saddle.

"That's not like you."

No. It wasn't.

"Doesn't have anything to do with how good-looking he is, does it?"

Alana glanced around quickly for Rana. She was out of hearing range, on the other side of the fence, holding open the gate for them all. "I'm not even going to answer that question." She clucked her horse forward.

"I've heard the buckle bunnies talking," Cabe said as he rode alongside her.

She had, too.

And that was exactly why she wanted no part of the man. He might be done with rodeo, but she had a feeling rodeo wouldn't be done with him. Men in his position usually went to work for the Professional Rodeo Association in some capacity. He'd be on the road 24/7, not exactly boyfriend material. Besides, she would never leave Rana. Never. The girl had already lost enough people in her young life.

Boyfriend?

"I'm not interested in Trent Anderson," she told Cabe. "So you can get that idea right out of your head."

Cabe just shrugged. "If you say so."

"I say so," she firmly told him.

She just wished she believed her own words.

Chapter Five

Frustrated.

The word summed up how Trent felt two days later. The damn woman wouldn't leave him alone. She kept strapping him onto a dang horse, insisting that he could use his hips better, clamp down with his thighs harder, use his lower leg to kick Baylor forward faster. He had rub marks on his calves and bruises on the insides of his thighs.

Today she agreed to take it easier on him, but only after he'd almost fallen out of his wheelchair after yesterday's particularly grueling session. They would work on leg-strengthening today, she'd told him, and resume riding the next day.

He couldn't wait.

A knock on the door sent his mood plummeting even more. "Enter."

She swung the door wide, pretty blue eyes scanning the interior of his cabin as if worried he might be hiding from her. He wasn't. He sat in his chair, which he'd positioned near the doorway of bedroom.

She smiled when she saw him. "Ready?"

Such a beautiful smile. Too bad she was a slave driver.

"Depends on what you have planned for me."

The smile grew wider. "Actually, we're going on a picnic."

If she'd told him they were flying to Mars, she couldn't have surprised him more. "A picnic is your idea of therapy?"

"Yup." She motioned him forward. "Come on. I'll show you."

She turned and left him standing there, a habit of hers, he'd noticed. The woman waited for no one, least of all him.

"Just a sec." He grabbed his cowboy hat off the peg by the door. He turned back to the front door in time to spot her scooping up a basket, a breeze throwing back the smell of fried chicken and...pie? Was that what he smelled?

His stomach grumbled.

"What is that?"

"Lunch."

He hadn't eaten all morning. Frankly, he'd been too exhausted to do much more than sleep.

"Can we eat here?"

She glanced back at him. "Nope. Where we're going isn't far."

"Smells good," he grumbled.

His chair picked up speed as he rolled toward her. She wore a red shirt this morning, one that emphasized a natural bloom on her cheeks. Her black hair had been left loose, and Trent had observed her enough times to know that she preferred it that way. She liked to flick it out of her face when she was determined to make him do something, which was pretty often, he admitted, his eye catching sight of her rear end, or more specifically, the crystal beads on her pockets. They caught the light and beamed out rainbow-colored prisms. Pretty jeans for a pretty woman.

Now, now. Just because she's taking it easy on you today is no reason to have thoughts like that.

A blind man would notice how gorgeous she was. The woman might be a termagant, but she was a good-looking termagant. And even though he might despise her militant attitude, she knew exactly what to say to motivate him into action. He respected that.

"How many guests can you accommodate here?"

The words caused her to slow down, Trent finally able to

stare at her profile. That was good. The view from the rear was entirely too distracting for his peace of mind.

"Eight families." She glanced down at him and Trent found himself wondering if maybe he should have kept quiet. When she wasn't giving him orders, he had a hard time focusing on her words because suddenly he was noticing how her eyes matched the color of the sky, and how the red shirt tucked into her jeans made her waist seem smaller.

"Most of the cabins sleep four people," she added when he kept quiet. "Although two of them, the ones on the end—" she pointed to the last two cabins "—they're bigger and can comfortably sleep six."

He couldn't care less, but if he were honest with himself, he could admit to feeling more relaxed. Between the light breeze on his face, the quiet gurgle of the river to his right and the pleasant tone of her voice, Trent found himself relaxing for the first time in ages.

"How long has this place been a guest ranch?"

"Since a year after Kimberly died."

The girl's mother, he thought. Alana's fiancé had died in the same wreck. Wait. She'd corrected him on that. She hadn't been engaged to Braden, but they'd been close, despite her words to the contrary. He thought about the emotions on her face when he questioned her the first day. The pain he'd spotted. The lingering sadness. The emptiness. He'd felt like a heel the moment he'd closed the door behind her.

"Is that how all this started? With Rana's injuries from the wreck?"

He saw her swallow and nod. "We almost lost her."

One of his wheels hooked on a rock. He straightened himself out before asking, "How long was she in the hospital?"

"Months." She shook her head, as if trying to shake off the memories. "She lost her mom and her uncle all in one fell swoop, and then had to fight for her life. It was almost too much for her to bear."

Was she speaking of Rana? Or herself?

"When we brought her home, Cabe and I put our heads together. I'd always planned on being a therapist, had the majority of my schooling done. He was desperate to get Rana back. The extent of her injuries harmed her mind as well as her body and so we came up with a plan to distract her. Horses. Lots and lots of horses. We made sure she was out of doors every chance we could get. I finished my degree and went to work on her. I guess you could say she was my guinea pig."

She'd slowed down, stopping by a massive tree, one with roots jutting out all the way down to the riverbank. A frog croaked nearby. The breeze had kicked up, and it tossed her hair back. She seemed lost in her thoughts. He almost didn't want to breathe for fear of distracting her. Then she blinked, met his gaze.

"Everything happens for a reason."

She meant the ranch, of course, not what he'd gone through.

"You didn't stop with Rana, though," he said.

"No. When word got out that Rana was walking again, the phone started ringing. Cabe talked to me about opening a guest ranch specializing in people with disabilities. I thought it was a great idea. We started looking into grants. Before we knew it, we had the financing and a waiting list. We couldn't build the cabins fast enough."

He could tell she loved what she did. Just talking about it set her whole face aglow, causing Trent to marvel at how pretty she was all over again. The sadness was gone and in its wake was the joy of her success.

"It seems quiet here now."

She smiled ruefully. "The calm before the storm. School's still in session. Come July we'll be packed solid. Cabe will bring in some help, usually interns from nearby colleges. It's crazy, but it's so amazing to watch people with a disability get on a horse for the first time. When they feel a horse beneath them, when they realize they can walk again, well, not them, but the horse, their faces light up. And then when they learn to control the horse and suddenly they're mobile in a way they never imagined…"

He could watch the play of emotions on her face all day. The happiness. The excitement. The satisfaction. He couldn't look away.

"I can't imagine ever leaving this place…or Rana. She's like a daughter to me now."

Suddenly, he was unaccountably jealous of Rana, and that was just plain ridiculous. Why?

Because she could walk again.

"How long did it take?"

She seemed to snap back to earth. "For what?"

"To teach Rana to walk again?"

She smiled. "Months, but Rana makes it sound like it took a decade. I've never seen anyone attack therapy like Rana did. She told me at one point that God might have taken her mother, but He wasn't going to take her legs away, too. She was angry." Alana stared at him pointedly. "We had to deal with that, too. I've learned it's pretty common for people to latch on to their anger when they've been dealt a debilitating blow."

The way he had. He couldn't miss her point.

"By the way, this is where we're having our picnic." She pointed to a spot beneath a tree, one so big its branches hung out over the nearby river. "That rope there will be your therapy today."

She'd done that on purpose, he realized—changed the subject.

"We'll work on leg strengthening, but not until after you eat."

When she opened the basket he once again caught a whiff of something fried and mouthwatering.

"Don't people think it strange, you living all the way out here with only Cabe and Rana for company?"

Her hands froze in the middle of unpacking plates. "No. Everyone knows we're just friends. But even if people did talk, I wouldn't care. I stick around as much for Rana as for myself. People can say what they want to say."

She wasn't messing around with Cabe—had never messed around with the man. He could see that in her eyes.

"Eat up." She handed him a plate full of food before sitting down next to the basket.

It was good. Delicious, actually. "You're a good cook."

"Thanks," she muttered, taking a bite of her own food. She didn't eat all daintylike, either. She ate like a woman who worked hard for a living and consumed calories to keep her energy.

Sexy.

He jerked his gaze away. What the hell was wrong with him? Okay, granted, she was hot. A year ago he would have crammed down his hat and gone after her. A year ago he'd have been able to pursue her. A year ago he'd had the use of his legs.

The thought put him in a sour mood all over again, the two of them eating in silence. He thought about making small talk, but what was the use? He didn't want to be her friend. Hell, he didn't want to be here at all. So if she insisted on dragging him out of his cabin, she could deal with the silence.

As it turned out, she didn't seem to care. As the silence stretched on, Trent found himself starting to relax again. That was, until she stuffed her plate back into the basket and asked, "Ready to get to work?"

He lost his appetite.

"Not really."

She smiled. He hated when she did that. It increased the wattage of her beauty, and he didn't like being in enemy territory.

"Too bad."

He glanced down at his own plate, surprised to note he'd eaten it all.

"Come on." She held out her hand for his plate. He reluctantly gave it to her. "Wheel yourself as close to the rope as you can get."

He didn't want to. He really didn't. He could feel things from about midthigh upward, and those thighs told him he was done—sore as a castrated bull dragged to the fire.

"What do you want me to do?"

"Simple, really. Just wheel yourself close to the rope and pull yourself up."

He eyed the rope in question. The thing dangled down from the branch above him, one with a canopy of leaves so thick you couldn't even see through it. Why did he have a feeling this wouldn't be as simple as she made it sound?

"You sure it will hold my weight?"

She smirked. "Positive."

Okay, so he was stalling, but he was really sore. All he wanted to do was sit in the damn chair.

He reached for the thick hemp, the fibers biting into his palms. It was as wide as a candlestick and easy to handle. He didn't have any problem lifting himself up, either, but the minute he'd pulled himself out of his chair, she jerked the thing out from under him.

"Hey!"

"Won't do you any good if you sit back down."

He dangled there like a stupid monkey and all she did was smile. "What am I supposed to do? Hang here?"

"No. I want you to straighten up. Use your legs to stand, then try walking."

"I can't walk. I'll fall on my ass."

"No, you won't. Just use the rope for balance."

He took a deep breath, let go with one hand and slapped a palm farther up the rope. His legs dangled uselessly beneath him.

"Stupid." He didn't mean to say the word out loud, but it slipped from between his lips before he could stop it.

"There's nothing stupid about this. I've seen your file. I looked at your scans. There's no reason why you can't regain the use of your legs. You just need to learn to trust them."

His arms had begun to shake. He pulled himself up another notch.

"There," she said. "Now get your legs beneath you."

"Can't."

"Do it."

He tried moving them, but as always, all he could do was swing them a little. He had no control. Just useless lumps of meat.

She leaned closer to him. "Move them."

His heart pounded. His arms had started to hurt.

"No."

He fell. She caught him, somehow supporting his weight, though how she did it he had no idea.

She smelled good.

"Do it again."

"No."

She started to let him go. He flailed his arms for the rope. Once again he found himself dangling there.

"Now move."

"I can't, damn it."

His arms started to hurt all over again.

"Just try."

"I am."

How long he hung there, he didn't know, but he'd be damned if he let go again. Alas, his body had other ideas. His grip began to loosen. He froze.

And fell once again into her arms.

"That's it." He huffed. "I'm done. Get my chair."

Lord, she smelled good.

"I can't reach it and still hold on to you." She strained beneath his weight, he could tell. "Grab the rope."

"I don't have the strength to lift myself up."

"Yes, you do."

He tried moving his limbs. Surprisingly, they worked, so much so that when they kicked into action, his legs shot them both backward. Somehow, she managed to swing his body around, his butt landing heavily in his wheelchair.

"See. I told you. I can't do it!"

"You can," she said, stepping back and sounding as out of breath as he felt. "All you need is practice. Come on. Let's do it again."

"No."

She cocked her head sideways. "No?"

He tried to keep his voice level. "It's no use. I tried the same sort of exercises before coming here, not this one exactly, but close. Nothing's helped. You're wasting your time."

She stared down at him. He wondered if she'd push the issue. She didn't.

"I'm sorry you feel that way." She bent and picked up the picnic basket. "But I won't work with someone if they refuse to help themselves." She slung the thing over her arm. "You have a choice to make, Mr. Anderson. Either you do the exercises I prescribe, or you go home."

"Excuse me?"

"I don't like wasting my time with half-ass efforts."

"Half-ass?"

"So if you decide to stay, you will do exactly as I tell you to do. If you don't, have a nice life."

She turned away.

"Wait. That's it? You're just going to leave me here?"

"You know the way back to your cabin."

She spun around and walked backward. "If you decide to stay, be at the barn tomorrow morning. Nine o'clock."

"And if I don't?"

She smirked again. "Like I said. Have a nice life."

Chapter Six

He wouldn't show. Alana had bet Cabe her best pair of boots that Trent would leave. She'd even listened for the sound of a car come to pick him up yesterday, or maybe the bus, but she hadn't heard anything. Last night Cabe had told her Trent had hung out in his cabin all day.

"You're going to owe me your boots," Cabe said as he walked into the barn the next morning.

"He's still here?" She couldn't keep the shock out of her voice.

"Spoke to him this morning. Said he'd see you in an hour." Cabe glanced at his watch, his face obscured by his cowboy hat for a moment. "That means you have a half hour to tack up Baylor."

He hadn't left.

She had no idea why she felt so relieved. Having Trent gone from the ranch would be a blessing. Less of a headache. She could prep for the influx of guests they'd get at the end of the month. But no. The stubborn cuss hadn't left.

"I'll be damned," she muttered.

Rana joined them in the barn, the girl excited about hanging out with her hero again. But when Trent arrived, Alana thought if his face had been a palette, it would have been painted in angry colors. Red. Black. Sienna. They were all there as he came to a stop near the barn's breezeway.

"Let's get to it," he said, not looking her in the eye.

"Mount up," she told him.

It was Rana who helped him onto his horse, and Rana who kept him company as they all rode out. Alana hung back, observing him, wondering about the best way to help him. Such a stubborn, hardheaded man.

"Do you see that?" Cabe asked, riding up alongside her.

They'd made it to the farthest edge of pasture, the part that began to slope upward, gradually giving way to pine trees and BLM land up above. The view, as usual, was spectacular, with the snow-covered mountains in the distance and the blue sky above. It had finally warmed up.

"If you mean the way his legs are flexing, then, yes, I had noticed."

From in front of them, they could hear Rana coaching Trent on how to control Baylor with his hips and hands, and Alana would have to admit, he did seem to be trying harder today. He'd been slowly getting the hang of it as they rode the fence line, checking on the level of grass. In the distance, the cows had spotted them, their steady mooing signaling their desire for more food, a definite sign that it was time to move them.

"His mom said scans indicate he should have more control over his lower limbs than he does." Cabe looked thoughtfully at their only guest.

"I read that in his file, too," Alana admitted.

Cabe glanced at her quickly.

"What?" She frowned. "I read all my patients' files. You know that. I also know they've been trying to coax him to continue with therapy for months. Now that I've seen his attitude, I know why. The man's so eaten up with bitterness he can't even see straight."

She watched as Trent moved his hips, his boot-clad heel lifting as he did so, and not because he'd shifted his weight in the saddle. It was more than that.

"So you think it might be psychological?" he asked.

Alana shrugged, her dark bay horse lifting its head as if

anticipating the cue for trotting. "I'm not sure. These injuries. Well, you know…it's not an exact science."

They'd learned that all too well with Rana. The doctors had said she'd never walk again. But the doctors had underestimated the determination of a ten-year-old girl who lived and breathed horses.

"You're going to keep pushing him, aren't you?" Cabe asked.

"I think I should," Alana said, but as they rode toward the back end of the pasture, her mind chewed over the problem. If he *did* have partial use of his lower extremities, that was a good sign, and a definite indication that his issues might be more mental than physical. The problem was how to get the man to cooperate. Still, she knew when to push and when to keep a low profile. She hung back today, letting Rana work with him, her mind spinning.

A half hour later Cabe called out to Rana, telling her it was time to head back. An hour on horseback. That was a good start. But as the teenager and her sidekick rode toward them, she found herself sliding alongside Trent, despite telling herself it might be wiser to leave him alone today. Rana took the hint and joined her father.

"How you feeling?" She made sure to give him the full force of her smile, not that it appeared to have any effect. She had a feeling if he'd been a dog, he would have growled.

"Fine."

He was still mad about yesterday. Okay. She understood that. He was still here, though, so that meant something.

"Your arms sore from yesterday?"

"No."

She held on to her patience by a spiderweb thread. The man made her grit her teeth. Worse, he made her seriously self-conscious. Every time she looked into his eyes it took an effort to keep her cheeks from blazing brightly. Why did he have to be so good-looking?

"Didn't your doctors tell you that you should be able to walk?"

There. She'd said it, although she instantly regretted the words. If he'd wanted to growl at her before, he wanted to bite her hand off now. He thrust his hips forward, hard, but Baylor refused to go faster. She almost smiled at the frustrated glare he shot her.

"Going somewhere?" she asked, knowing it would infuriate him further but wanting to rattle his cage for some reason.

"Obviously," he hissed, "there's no chance of me ever walking again. I would have thought you'd realized that yesterday. I can't even get this damn horse to move."

"Yes, you can."

Anger. Bitterness. Frustration. She saw all that in his eyes and more.

"Are you afraid of failing?" Harsh, yes, but the question needed to be asked.

"I'm not afraid of anything."

"Good," she said quickly. "Because I've been taking it easy on you up until today. Not anymore."

His head whipped back around, brows low, gray eyes glittering. "What?"

"The sooner we dig in, the better."

She reached out and grabbed one of his reins. He tried to jerk them away.

"What are you doing?"

"We're going to trot."

"No, we are not." He tried to pull the reins back. "I'll fall."

"Not in that saddle." She smiled at him, but kept a firm grip on the single rein. "All you have to do is hang on."

"No."

But Baylor knew what to do. The moment she clucked her horse into a trot, the animal followed.

"Stop."

It was the worst part of her job—pushing people when they didn't want to be pushed. She consoled herself, as she always did, by telling herself this was good for him. He didn't believe he could ride, but he could in their specially made saddle. He could even gallop if he'd put in a little effort learning Baylor's cues. He was just being stubborn.

So as she trotted off, she ignored his cries of protest. She didn't look in his direction, either, certain all she'd see was anger in his eyes. The soft footfalls of Baylor's hooves matched her own horse's steps. After a few yards, she risked a glance backward, wanting to see if he was bouncing out of the saddle or sitting quietly.

Sitting quietly.

She turned away before he could see the smile breaking across her face. Ah. The man might be holding on to the saddle's horn like a drowning victim, but he wasn't moving, a sure sign that his legs still functioned.

They caught up to Rana and Cabe in a matter of seconds, Alana pulling her horse and Trent's to a stop.

"Whew, I'm getting hungry," she told the group at large, letting go of Baylor's reins. "I'm thinking BLTs for lunch."

Rana chirped a resounding "Yes." Cabe just smiled. Trent glared.

She should have expected it, she really should have, but it was a bit of a disappointment to realize he was so deep into his self-pity he hadn't even noticed how well he'd clung to his horse.

And then he leaned toward her. Alana pulled up her horse, slowing it down so Rana and Cabe wouldn't hear what Trent said. It was a good thing, too.

"If you ever do that again, I swear, I will somehow find a blowgun and shoot your horse in the ass with a dart."

To which she just smiled. "Well, Mr. Anderson, I'd start combing eBay, then, because I plan to do a lot of stuff like that over the next two weeks." She'd already wasted one week taking it easy on him. Not anymore.

Before he could say another word, she clucked to her horse and cantered away.

AN HOUR LATER Trent still fumed. He could have fallen and been killed today.

And wouldn't that have been poetic?

Killed by a horse and not that stupid drunk driver.

He couldn't leave fast enough. Trent ignored the scenic view once he shot out of the barn. The pine trees weren't as thick as they were at the edge of the Jensen property, but they still afforded some shade from the sun as he traveled along the gravel path. Some days he wished he were a vampire, a being that would simply poof out of existence in the sun's rays.

The path wound through a small meadow with loamy red earth smelling musty and dank, and birds chirping in the trees. One thing about the world, no matter how much crap you were wading in, the damn thing still turned. So did the wheels of his chair, faster and faster, although this part of the property wasn't as steep a grade as the main road, it just took longer to navigate. Trent slowed down once he was out of view.

He wished he'd had the courage to leave yesterday. He couldn't. He'd promised his mom he'd try and stick it out for three weeks. His traitorous mother, who'd clearly handed over his medical records to the slave driver Alana. He couldn't believe she'd sold him out.

When he made it back to his cabin, his hands still shook, making it difficult to dial Saedra's number.

"I was wondering when you'd get around to calling me."

He smiled when he heard her voice, the first time he'd grinned in this godforsaken place since arriving. He wheeled his chair toward the giant picture window at the front of his cabin. Sunlight glinted off the nearby river. They appeared to be in a low-lying valley, one surrounded on all sides by small mountains, and in the distance to the northwest was what looked like a volcano covered in snow. Tall pine trees dotted the hills and turned them green. Pretty country, but nothing could beat the beauty of Colorado.

"Believe me. I was tempted to keep you in the dark," Trent said.

He hadn't exactly left Colorado on good terms with Saedra…
or his mom. If he hadn't been certain his mother would completely disown him if he called it quits, he would have left on
the first plane out of here.

"So, have they put you on a torture rack yet?"

He heard amusement in her voice. "They have me riding
in a rocking chair."

Despite his anger at being all but bullied by his new therapist, Trent's spirits lifted. He didn't like being on bad terms
with Saedra. They'd been through too much. After the car
wreck that'd taken his rodeo partner's life, Saedra had been
a rock, always by his side, urging him on. She'd taken time
away from her own thriving business to help nurse him back
to health. There was no way he could repay her for that, and
if he were honest with himself, it was part of the reason why
he'd come to California despite his reservations. Saedra had
put the guilt screws into him but good, telling him that after
everything she'd done for him, after all the time she'd spent
trying to get him well, he owed it to her to at least try one last
thing. So here he was.

"What?" He could hear Saedra's laughter. "What do you
mean a rocking chair?"

"It's the damn saddle they have me riding in. It's like a rocking chair. It even has a back."

"You *rode* today?"

Her words brought him back to the moment, back to the
point in time when he'd first climbed on his horse and nearly
broken into tears.

"I've actually ridden a few times."

"Oh, Trent."

Okay, fine. He would admit that it always felt good to get
back in the saddle. The only thing he didn't like was the harridan in charge of rehabilitating him.

"Don't sound so thrilled. It's not like I'm running barrels."

She was silent for a moment. He wondered where she was.
Probably still packing up the last of her things from the busi-

ness she'd sold. His accident had changed more than him. Saedra had watched her best friend struggle to survive, the whole
ordeal making her realize life was too short to put a dream on
hold—or so she'd told him. So she'd sold Buckaroo Barbecues,
her successful catering business in Denver, bought a trailer to
live in, and plotted her strategy on the best way to get to the
National Finals Rodeo herself.

At least some good had come out of this whole mess.

"No. I don't expect you did." She sounded sad. It annoyed
Trent to no end.

"I'll leave the barrel racing to you."

She was quiet for a moment. "I can't believe you rode."

"Yeah, well, I wouldn't have if it wasn't for the drill sergeant
of a therapist they have here at the ranch."

"Keeping you on your toes, huh?"

"I'm surprised she doesn't carry a bullwhip."

"Your therapist is a she?"

Why did he feel as if he shouldn't have revealed that little bit
of information? There was nothing between him and Saedra...
never had been. They were childhood friends. Yeah, sure, once
upon a time they'd tried dating. Their first kiss had been such a
disaster, they'd decided to never do it again, and they hadn't.

"She's *no* lady," Trent grumbled.

He heard soft laughter on the other end of the line. "I can
only imagine what she's like if she's already brought the devil
out in you. Does she know what she's in for?"

He moved back from the window, rolling his wheelchair
toward the kitchen one-handed. He didn't want to think about
Alana and the way she made him feel. He'd wanted to jump
off his horse and run, except he couldn't, and she knew that,
and it made him want to scream in frustration.

*Because she's the best-looking woman you've seen since
your days on the rodeo circuit.*

Back when he'd been a whole man, not half of one.

"She reminds me of you," Trent said, although he had no

idea where the words had come from. He didn't want to think about Alana. He really didn't.

"Me, huh? That can't be a good thing. Do you butt heads with her like you do me?"

"Oh, yeah."

On the bottom shelf of the fridge was a package of ham. He pulled it out, placing it on his lap. He did the same thing with some sliced cheese he found, and the mustard and mayonnaise, turning around and heading for the kitchen counter that had been built considerably lower than normal to accommodate people with special needs.

Special needs.

He hated the term. Hated it with a passion.

"I should get going." He placed the meat and condiments on the countertop.

"Yeah, I should, too. I have to finish loading the trailer, but it's so good to hear your voice."

She was at home, getting ready to hit the road, something he'd never do again. Suddenly, he lost his appetite.

"Trent, promise me something, will you?"

His whole body stilled. The last time she'd asked to promise her something, he'd found himself on a plane to California a week later.

"Stick it out," she said when he didn't answer.

He closed his eyes. Unfortunately, when he did that, he could perfectly picture Saedra with her blond hair and blue eyes. She would be giving him the look. The one that made her eyes glisten with suppressed emotion: concern, sadness, determination.

A look a lot like the one Alana had given him yesterday, and then this morning when he'd trotted on Baylor.

"I'll try."

He hung up before she made him promise anything else, like trying to walk again…it would take a miracle for that to happen.

Chapter Seven

Go on. Knock.

Alana felt the breath she held begin to whistle past her lips.

So what if he makes you feel anxious and self-conscious? She'd worked with good-looking men before. Hell, that downhill skier they'd had last year had actually graced the covers of magazines.

Hadn't fazed her one bit.

So why Trent?

Taking another deep breath, she headed up the ramp, the tiny porch still in shadows, Alana thinking it was just about time to hang the flower baskets along the front. She smiled inwardly. As if a man like Trent would appreciate flower baskets.

Leaning forward, she listened for a few seconds. He might still be asleep. She leaned back, her hair falling over one shoulder. Oh, well. He would soon learn that it was "game on." From here on out it'd be an 8:00 a.m. start. She lifted her hand to knock.

The door opened.

Alana rocked back in surprise, her gaze dropping to the handsome son of a cuss sitting in a wheelchair.

Thank God he wore a shirt today.

Why do you always think that?

"You going to stand out there all day, or what?"

"Or what," she instantly quipped as, for about the tenth time since she'd met him, her skin turned various shades of red, her cheeks filling with warmth.

He wore a maroon button-down shirt this morning, his off-white cowboy hat back in place, denim jeans hugging a waistline that was still trim despite his injury.

"Did you need something?" he asked.

This wasn't going to work if she kept getting flustered whenever he was near. So she took a deep breath, pasted a smile on her face and said, "Time to get to work," in as happy a tone she could muster.

"Don't you believe in weekends off?"

Was it the weekend? She hadn't noticed.

"Not around here. I like to do my therapy all the time."

He didn't look pleased. She wondered if she'd have to goad him into complying.

"Thought I'd give you a ride." She pointed behind her shoulder to the Mule parked out behind her.

"I told you yesterday, no amount of therapy is going to help me get better."

"And I told you that I don't think that's true." Her smile slipped a notch. She jerked it back into place. "Do you need to grab anything before we go?"

"A pair of headphones so I don't have to listen to you."

Sarcasm. She'd expected that. "I was thinking more along the lines of something to eat. You're going to need your energy."

Gray eyes swept her up and down in a way that made her instantly uncomfortable. What would he see? A woman in her mid-twenties with windswept hair and dirt under her fingernails? And damn it all to hell, that pissed her off, because she shouldn't care what he saw. The man was a former rodeo star with enough baggage to fill a Mack truck. That was what she needed to focus on. Getting him better. Not how his dark blond good looks made her feel.

"I've already eaten." He wheeled himself backward.

"Where are you going?"

"I need to grab my jacket." He rotated his chair.

She slunk outside, grateful for the pine-scented air that cooled her cheeks. Or maybe it was his aroma that was so delicious.

Stop it.

She had to quit doing this. She had to start thinking of him as a client, not as one of the most handsome men she'd ever met.

"Let's go."

The wheels of his chair clattered down the ramp's wooden slats. She knew he was behind her, hated how self-conscious that made her feel. Was he staring at her butt? Did he think the jeans were too tight? They had rhinestones on the pockets. Cabe had given them the once-over when he'd spotted her earlier in the barn. And, sure, yeah, she hardly ever wore pretty clothes. She'd just felt like dressing up a little today. She'd donned a dark blue shirt with silver threads sewn into the fabric because she hardly ever wore them—she'd told Cabe that very thing.

"You don't need to give me a ride." He eyed the Mule as if there were snakes on the floorboard.

"It's faster if we take this."

She motioned for him to get inside.

"I need the exercise."

"You'll get plenty of that today."

Clearly, he didn't want to comply with her wishes. His mouth had compressed into a thin line, a muscle near his jaw ticking in frustration, his hands clenching, too, something she was beginning to realize signaled massive frustration on his part.

"Get in, Trent."

His eyes spouted flames. "Fine." He leaned forward, and the way he slashed at his wheels with his hands had to hurt. He didn't seem to notice. Clearly, he wasn't going to make this easy. Just as clearly, he wanted to save face. She would use that to her advantage.

He wheeled his chair up next to the Mule. His hands reached toward the seat, and he expertly shifted from the chair to the all-terrain vehicle. She took his chair away, folding it closed then storing it in the back. When she slipped into the driver's seat, the jaw muscle was still ticking, his hands still clenching.

"Look." She swiveled in her seat. "I realize you're pissed off at the world."

His gaze lashed toward her.

"And you have a right to be angry. Nobody likes going from the top cowboy in the nation to an invalid in a wheelchair, but get over it."

He wasn't used to such plain speaking. Or maybe he was. Either way he shot her a look of outrage.

"You're here to heal, and with any luck, to walk again, but as I've said before, that's not going to happen if you resist me at every turn."

"But that's the problem," he said softly. "I've already been down this road. Don't you get it? Nothing's going to change."

"I think you're wrong."

His face turned to stone, but at least he wasn't clenching his fists anymore. He had scars, deep ones, and she needed to probe them, if his inability to walk had anything to do with his mental state.

As gently as she could, she said, "It's not your fault Dustin didn't survive."

If she hadn't been staring closely at him, she would have missed the way his jaw flexed, wouldn't have noticed his shoulders jerking…as if she'd hit him. He didn't face her, but he didn't need to in order for her to see what was going through his mind.

"Accidents happen."

He said the words by rote, as if he'd been coached to say them.

"Yes, but survivor's guilt is a terrible thing."

Pain lined his face, causing his lips to tip down and the space between his eyes to wrinkle. He was lost in his memories for a moment, anguish briefly surfacing on his face before he shoved it away.

"Let's go."

Two little words, but it was clear he would brook no argument. She thought about pressing the matter, but only for a moment. In the end, her own sense of self-preservation won out.

"Hang on." She leaned forward and started the Mule's motor.

SHE TOOK HIM to the arena.

"I figure we'll do things a little differently than what you're used to." She slipped out of the Mule, unhooking his wheelchair from the back. "Since you did so well yesterday when trotting, we're going to try that again."

"I'm not riding." He was well aware he sounded like a petulant child, told himself he didn't care.

"Well, that's too bad. You're going to help me tack up the horses, too." She pointed with her thumb to the barn behind them.

"I'm not."

She pushed his chair up next to the Mule, patting the back of it. "Come on." She smiled. "Off we go."

He wasn't going to do it. It could be dangerous. A horse might do something unexpected, like twist around over the top of him.

"Come on." She patted the chair again.

Stick it out.

Damn Saedra. And damn his mother for sending him here.

He scowled, although it didn't appear to scare her, his hands pressing against the seat. He'd become an expert on swinging himself from the bed to his wheelchair, then his wheelchair to the couch, and on and on and on, the muscles in his arms more sculpted than they'd ever been. This was no different. He made quick work of moving from the chair to the Mule.

*Wheel*chair.

He closed his eyes against the sickness that welled up inside of him.

He was in a frickin' wheelchair.

It wasn't fair. He'd survived the wreck while Dustin had been flung—

Quickly, he shut down the thought. He hadn't lost consciousness. Not for one single second—and the smell of fuel and burned plastic was something he would never forget. Some days he could still smell the acrid stench, or so it seemed.

The breath he took shook with the effort to contain his emotions. He rested his arms on his wheelchair. His damned cage. A thing he hated more than anything in the world.

"Good job."

He was surprised she didn't pat him on the head as if he was a kid or something. He wasn't that. He'd spent the past six months learning how to be self-sufficient. He could dress himself. Bend down without falling out of his chair to tie his laces. He could even slip in and out of a bathtub. And he'd learned how to do all that because he didn't like feeling like a child—even if he might sound like one sometimes.

"I'm not helping with the horses." He drew the line at that.

"Too bad." She stepped away from his chair. At least she didn't try to push him. He hated when people felt as if they had to "help" him. "It's part of your therapy."

"I'd rather do traditional therapy."

Except, suddenly, he didn't. Traditional therapy meant someone touching him. He didn't want anyone doing that. Not anymore.

Especially not a good-looking someone.

"That's not an option today." She punctuated her words with a bright smile, one that set her blue eyes aglow and emphasized the height of her cheekbones. She could model, this woman.

She headed toward the stable, leaving him behind. He faced the same decision he'd faced the other day. Either he went along with this craziness, or he turned around, packed up his bags and left California far behind.

Anderson men don't shy away from anything.

Damn her. Damn Saedra. Damn his mother.

"Slow down," he called out to her, figuring he was here, so

he might as well see what happened. With any luck, a horse would run him down and he'd get injured and sent home.

He should only be so lucky.

Chapter Eight

She had to give him credit. He was sticking it out.

"Here." She tossed him Baylor's lead rope. Trent snatched it from the air, but not before shooting her a deer-in-the-headlights look. "Tie him up outside."

"I can't lead a horse from my wheelchair."

She turned around in the middle of the barn aisle, walking backward. "One thing you should learn. We don't like the word *can't* around here."

She headed toward Radical's stall, the dark bay gelding nickering to her. "Ready to work, Mr. R.?" she asked the horse, glancing back and noting that Trent hadn't moved. Baylor stood near him, head held low, ears tipping backward and forward, the animal clearly puzzled about what he was supposed to do.

"Turn around and lead the horse out, Trent."

She grabbed her own horse's halter, slipping inside the stall before he could complain again or think of another reason why he shouldn't be asked to do such a menial task.

She thought she heard him say, "If I get killed..."

She smiled. The man was full of complaints. At this rate, it'd be dinnertime before they rode.

He appeared proud of himself when she led Radical outside. Trent had rolled away from the hitching post, and Baylor stood quietly nearby.

"Well, look at that," she drawled. "Looks like you could do it after all."

"Bite me."

She whirled to face him. "Excuse me?"

"I said bite me."

She bit back a smile. This was more like it. She'd rather him be snarky and snarly than full of self-pity and self-loathing. Anything was better than that.

"Grab a brush. Get to work. If you get thirsty, there's an office upstairs with a fridge. I can grab you something to drink."

"What if the horse pushes me over?"

"He's not going to push you over." She finished tying Radical to the rail. "That horse has seen more people in wheelchairs than a handicapped parking spot. Now get busy."

She didn't glance back at him again, just busied herself with her own horse, removing shavings from his mane, picking his feet, checking to make sure there were no bumps or bruises from his night in the stall.

"Done," she heard him say.

She was half tempted to tell him to go grab the saddle, but she wasn't that cruel—and it would be cruel. She might pretend otherwise, but there *was* a limit to what he could do. Maybe one day he could balance the saddle on his lap while he navigated the ramp, but not today.

She chirped the word *great* and went to get what he'd need.

"I'm not riding in that armchair thing," he said as she walked by.

"You'll ride in it if I tell you to."

"I want a regular saddle." She heard him roll up behind her when she turned back, dust mixed with early morning sunlight to shroud his shape. With his arms resting on his wheels, he looked like a gunslinger, his gray eyes blazing as brightly as the sun behind him.

"You're not ready for a regular saddle."

"Then I guess I don't ride."

He could really get his back up, she thought. But at least she wasn't drooling all over him and blushing like a teenager. She almost argued the point, but decided, what the heck? He might not want to believe it, but he had more use of his legs than he thought. He really shouldn't need the specialty saddle.

"Fine."

She saw his eyes widen, saw him lean back in his chair as if she'd literally blown him away. Once again she found herself biting back a smile. Maybe this wouldn't be so bad after all. Maybe this might be fun.

She used a buckaroo saddle, one with a deep seat and a high cantle in the back. The horn was double the size of a regular saddle, too.

More for him to grab on to.

He didn't complain. She finished quickly, Trent watching the whole time.

"Go on." She motioned toward the ramp. "Head on over. I'll load him into the stocks."

He glared. She smiled again. Yup, this would be fun, although maybe not so much fun for him. He looked a little intimidated when he made it to the top of the ramp and faced the western saddle. No strap. Nothing to catch him if he made a wrong move. Frankly, she wondered if she shouldn't go and get the other saddle—to hell with his pride.

Oh, yeah, and Trent would like that about as much as a bad case of poison ivy.

She heard herself say, "Careful," even though she hadn't meant to say anything.

He must have taken the word as a challenge, because he leaned forward and pulled himself into the saddle in the blink of an eye. He'd swung his leg around and straddled the horse so smoothly he looked as though he'd been doing it for months.

"Good job."

She tossed the reins at him. He caught them and, unlike yesterday, didn't protest when she turned away. She didn't mount her horse, though. Instead she led her horse toward the arena, the white wooden rail looking extrabright in the afternoon sunlight. She heard Trent follow. Good, she thought, opening the gate. They were lucky; their arena was state-of-the-art. There were even two identical chutes to the left of the gate, and an alleyway outside so they could load the cattle for roping, and a stripping chute to the back of the arena. All of it was for Cabe and Rana's benefit when they practiced. Opposite the gate, on the far side, they'd built a shed. Inside was an assortment of pylons and barrels and…there it was. She dropped the reins, Radical standing patiently as he'd been trained to do, and Trent pulled up his own horse.

"What the hell is that?" she heard him say.

"It's a soccer ball."

Only it wasn't. Not really. The oversized ball was as big as a beanbag chair…maybe bigger, but it had the black-and-white hexagonal patches in the tradition of a soccer ball. Alana kicked the thing toward Trent. He straightened as if expecting his horse to spook. Baylor didn't.

"We're going to play a little game." She went to the shed, pulling out pylons this time. In a matter of minutes, she had goalposts set up at either end of the arena.

"You've got to be kidding," he said.

When she met his gaze, his expression was one of dismay mixed with horror.

She threw the reins over her horse's neck. "You're a competitive individual, Trent. I'm betting that once I kick your booty a few times, you'll get into the spirit of the game."

"You're crazy."

"Nope." She swung herself up, patting her horse as a reward for standing patiently, then she picked up the reins. "I'm your therapist." She wiggled in the saddle. "And I won't take it easy on you anymore. Now. Let's say we make this a little more interesting."

He was sitting in the saddle pretty well for a man who claimed to have lost all feeling in his legs, she noticed. He hadn't lost his balance once on their way to the arena. That was telling all on its own.

"How about a little wager?"

He peered at her from beneath the brim of his hat. "You're going to bet against a man in a wheelchair."

"That's just it." She clucked her horse forward. "You're not in a wheelchair. You have four good legs beneath you, so use them."

She had a feeling if he'd had a fly swatter he would have used it on her. She'd be nothing more than a flattened mass of blackness.

"That's the problem." He lifted his reins. "I can't control the four legs beneath me."

"You'll learn."

She was being harsh. She knew that, just as she knew it was for his own good. Sometimes a therapist had to put on the mean-girl panties. This was one of those times.

"Okay." She turned her horse toward the ball. "There's only one rule. No loping or cantering. Trot only. Goals are on either side of the arena, and either one of them counts. Winner gets to ask the loser for something."

"What something?"

"Anything."

His eyes narrowed. "I would wish for your head to explode."

She turned back, startled into a laugh. "Maybe you'll get your wish. Come on."

She kicked Radical into a fast trot. The horse headed straight for the ball. Trent was left behind. Alana caught a glimpse of his face when she rounded the other side of the ball and faced the goal about a hundred feet away. Outrage. Frustration, and then the expression she'd been hoping for.

Determination.

He took the reins and slapped his horse with them. Alana gasped, prepared to ride to his rescue, but any fear she had that his legs really were useless was banished the moment Baylor jerked forward and Trent clung to the saddle just fine.

A sigh of relief rushed past her lips. And, okay, maybe he wasn't the prettiest rider in the world. He was a long way from what he used to be, something that filled her with momentary sadness. He kept himself horse-bound by sheer force of will. His knuckles were white, they gripped the saddle horn so tightly. His upper body was hunched forward, too, his legs flapping a bit, sure, but not anywhere near as much as she would have expected from a true paraplegic.

She closed he eyes in relief. *Thank You, Lord.*

She let him get close enough to give him hope before clucking Radical forward so that the horse's knees kicked the ball out of his way.

"Ooh," she groaned, their two horses brushing past each other. Baylor was a veteran soccer player, but the horse took care to keep Trent safe. "So close."

He somehow managed to let go of the horn long enough to pull on the reins. He didn't say anything, but he didn't need to, because she could see the frustration in his eyes.

"Tell you what," she called as the ball dribbled to a stop a few feet away. "First person to hit five goals wins, and I'll spot you a two-goal advantage."

"I don't need an advantage."

"No?" She kicked her horse forward again, calling out over her shoulder, "Your loss."

Radical knew how the game was played, too, the horse hardly slowing down as he trotted up to the giant ball, one of his front legs striking the ball square in the middle and sending it flying. She didn't look back to see how Trent was doing as she pulled her horse up, turning him and lining him up with the ball so that the next hit would send it sailing through the pylons. With a cluck and a kick the ball flew forward again.

"Ooh! Score."

She turned around in time to see Trent trotting up behind her, looking like a monkey clinging to a dog's back, but he was still on board. He wasn't slowing down, either. No. The man headed straight for the ball on the other side of the goalpost.

Yes!

Just as she'd hoped. His competitive spirit had kicked in. And, honestly, he was poised to kick the ball right at her. Surprise held her immobile as Baylor smoothly faced the ball and then kicked it right toward her.

"Hey," she said. "I thought you said you couldn't ride."

Was that a smile on his face? Okay, maybe it was a teeny-weeny one, but she would take anything at this point.

She pointed Radical toward the ball. The race was on from that point forward. Baylor was a bigger horse with a bigger step. Trent caught up with her quickly, but she reached the ball first, Radical kicking the thing out of his way, but she didn't get there first by much. Trent's horse played the game all on its own so all Trent had to do was hang on. And he did, but she still scored the point before him, with Radical kicking the thing so hard it bounced off the fence and back toward the middle of the arena again.

"Sure you don't want an advantage?" She pulled Radical up.

"No."

Wow. He was a tough nut to crack. "Okay, then. Three–zip."

And they were off again, but Trent had the advantage, and Baylor knew exactly what to do. The horse kicked the ball toward the other side of the arena in an explosive move that sent it straight toward the goal.

"Good one," she cried, trotting toward the far side of the arena. "Three to one."

She almost scored another goal, mostly because the ball bounced in her favor, but Trent was right on it. Alana was surprised to realize she was enjoying herself. She had no idea how he managed to balance atop Baylor so well, but somehow he did. Probably his years of riding bulls. He had way more muscle control than he thought, and he scored a goal to prove it.

She scored the next goal, but Trent anticipated the ball's bounce so that he was poised perfectly to capitalize on the ricochet, and Baylor hit the ball so that it bounced through the goals, hit the arena fence, then bounced back toward her.

"Not fair." She pretended to frown, but inside she did back-flips. Good for him.

"Four to four," he called out, turning Baylor around. She

realized he might just beat her to the ball if she didn't get a move on.

She turned Radical around. They both raced toward the ball. In seconds he was on her, the two of them neck and neck. Baylor edged ahead, but her own horse's competitive nature kicked in, the animal extending the trot. He struck it first, the ball propelled forward by the force of Radical's left leg. She glanced at Trent, nearly pulling her horse up when she spotted him slipping to the side. Instead of slowing down, Trent urged Baylor onward, and Alana wondered if she might actually lose the match. His lack of balance was his undoing. She saw him clutch at the reins; Baylor instantly slowed. She surged ahead. It was all over then. With a mighty push, the ball went flying toward the pylons.

"Hah!" She lifted her hands in victory. "Nothing but net."

"You got lucky."

"Yes, I did." She pointed. "And you didn't fall off."

"Because bull riding has taught me to hang on with my hands."

And how to balance with his still-working thighs, but she had seen his calves clench the side of the horse, too. Sure, it might be related to the movement of the horse, but what if it wasn't? What if she really did have more to work with than Trent let on?

"You owe me a favor."

To give him credit, he didn't balk. He'd pulled up alongside her, straightening in the saddle once he'd stopped, wincing a bit as he threw his shoulders back.

"What could you possible want from me?"

The unspoken words were *someone who's crippled and useless*.

"I want you to give Rana lessons."

He frowned, clearly perplexed. "Lessons?"

"She's a breakaway roper. One of the best in the county. I'd like you to help her improve."

He immediately shook his head. "Impossible. I would need

to ride alongside of her." He leaned forward, as if he feared she might miss his next words. "*Run* alongside of her. I could barely hang on at a trot."

"Bull. You can coach her from the sidelines."

"That's a half-ass way of doing it." Sunlight hit his face head-on, illuminating the dent in his square chin and dazzling eyes. He sat his horse just like any other cowboy, and Alana was reminded of the cover photo she'd seen of him once upon a time, on some rodeo magazine, the man photographed just as he was now. Square in the saddle, one hand resting on the horn, the other holding the reins.

Handsome.

"Look, maybe you don't think it's a big deal, but to her it will be the most amazing experience of her life. She idolizes you, Trent. Didn't you notice that yesterday? She would do anything for you. I'm hoping you'll do something for her."

His eyes dimmed a bit, Alana spotting something that might just be shame.

"She competes?" he asked.

"Every chance she gets. She's going to make it to the High School Rodeo Finals, or at least that's the plan. I'm hoping you could help her get there."

"I don't know what you think I can do."

She rode up to him, her leg brushing against his, though he didn't seem to notice. She did, though. She felt the connection all the way to her bones.

"You're one of the world's best cowboys. You *are,* Trent," she insisted when she noticed the doubt on his face. "You might be a little down-and-out right now, but you still have it all right here." She pointed to her head. "There's a wealth of information up there just waiting to be shared. Please." She leaned forward, rested a hand on his thigh. "Stop thinking of yourself as useless. You aren't. You are a vibrant, talented, healthy male."

Boy, was he ever male. She could smell the sweat on him, the combination of man and horse causing her to pull back some.

"She's been having trouble lately, and we can't figure it out. All it takes is one piece of advice, just one thing none of us might have thought of that you would spot right off the bat. Maybe that her horse is sore. Maybe she's jerking on the reins. Maybe her horse isn't running straight. I don't know. My point is we need your eyes, and last I checked, those worked just fine."

He had the good grace to look ashamed. He turned away for a moment, his face in profile, and she could tell her words had gotten through to him. Finally. Now, if she could just forget about how he smelled, things would be even better.

"What time do you want to do this?"

She almost lifted her hands in victory again. Hallelujah and praise the Lord.

"How about after dinner? That gives you the rest of the day to relax."

"Fine."

She leaned toward him again, and though she told herself not to do it, though she knew it was a terribly forward thing to do, she couldn't seem to stop from brushing his cheek with her lips. He smelled so good, she hovered for a moment, simply absorbing the scent of him.

What are you doing? You're his therapist. For goodness' sake, Alana, don't make this personal.

She centered herself in the saddle again, her cheeks ablaze.

"I, um…aah. Thanks, Trent. This will mean a lot to her. Maybe you're no longer the hero of the rodeo circuit, but you can be a hero to someone like Rana."

His eyes had widened from her kiss. She looked away, even more embarrassed.

"Let's get you off that horse," she said before she did something else impulsive, like take his hand and squeeze it.

"Yeah, let's."

Chapter Nine

Trent didn't want to go…but he had to.

He knew that, had lectured himself the whole way to the stables. So what if she'd kissed him? She hadn't meant anything by it. He knew that. Had been able to tell by the look on her face that she didn't think of him that way.

What way?

He felt his cheeks heat. The way he *wanted* her to think of him. The way he'd fantasized—as a man, one she found attractive and desirable.

The man he used to be.

"Where do you want me?" Trent asked as he slowly rolled to a stop near the entrance of the barn. Trent and Alana stood near a red roan horse that Rana was in the middle of saddling.

"Wherever you want," Alana said with a smile.

"Trent," Cabe said, nodding.

"Cabe." He met Alana's gaze again. "I'll be out by the arena."

He wheeled himself away before she could say another word. It was unreal what her kiss had done to him. And it'd just been a kiss on the cheek. Like dangling off a high-voltage wire, that's what it was like. Hair on end. Skin charged by energy. All because she'd pressed her lips against him.

Damn it.

He made it to the arena without embarrassing himself, his gaze scanning for a place to watch. No ramp for a handicapped person. No platform for spectators. Great. If he wheeled himself into the middle of arena, he'd tip over.

"You can watch from over there," Alana said a few minutes later. Trent turned back in time to see her smiling face again, her long dark hair mussed, the matching lashes perfectly setting off her light eyes.

Gorgeous.

She pointed. "There's a little berm over there."

For people in wheelchairs.

She didn't need to point out the obvious. His face colored, and he wheeled himself away again. Even just wearing a pair of jeans and an off-white button-down top, she looked sexy.

Shoving his hat down low, he told himself so what if she'd kissed him? It hadn't meant anything. The woman had just been grateful. That was all. Nothing more.

"What do you want me to do?"

The question came from Rana, who'd ridden over to his side, the horse she rode the color of a strawberry smoothie. Good-looking animal. Low to the ground, stocky and pretty energetic based on the way it danced around.

"Let me see you break from the box a few times."

He saw Rana frown, and he could have sworn her shoulders slumped, but she turned her horse toward the gate and the roping chute nonetheless. The moment she entered the twelve-by-twelve area, the animal began to balk.

Rana pulled back on the reins. "Whoa, whoa, whoa."

He could tell it was all the girl could do to keep the horse pointed in the right direction.

Okay. So that wasn't going to work. Was that why Alana had begged him to work with her?

"Why don't we forget the box for now?" Trent called out. "Just circle him in the arena."

She was trying to turn the animal, but the more she tried, the more the horse became wound up, half rearing at one point.

"Is he always like this?" Trent asked when Cabe and Alana joined him.

"Never used to be," Alana said, her blue eyes troubled. She flicked her hair back over her shoulder. "But lately…"

They all watched as Rana tried to soothe the animal; all attempts failed. When she turned Scooter toward the box once more, the animal spun on his hoofs and bolted.

"Whoa," he heard her cry out.

The horse ignored her. It wasn't until she made it to the other end that she finally got him slowed down.

"We've tried everything." Cabe appeared troubled, too, his eyes narrowing as he watched his daughter. "For the past week she's just been walking around the arena. Hasn't even tried getting him near the box."

Alana, next to him, shook her head. "It hasn't helped."

She lifted a foot and placed it on the bottom rail, the jeans she wore stretching across her rear and cupping her—

Trent!

Man. What was wrong with him? He acted like a man who'd never been around a woman before.

Forcing himself to focus, he tried to keep his gaze trained on Rana. He would have to give the girl credit. She was one hell of a rider. She clung to the gelding like a burr, turning Scooter around by sheer force of will. The animal tried bolting back to the gate, but she held him tight, her knuckles whitening as she clutched the reins. The roan horse's veins popped, his hooves kicking up sand and leaving behind tiny dust clouds, eyes wild.

"Has he been like this at competitions, too?"

Alana nodded, but she wasn't paying any attention to him. It took everything Trent had to keep his eyes off her rear end and on Rana, not that Alana would have noticed his ogling her. Her gaze was focused on Rana, and he could tell she was crestfallen.

"It's okay, honey," she called out.

When the girl got nearer, he could see she fought back tears. *Okay. Focus.*

He'd dealt with this problem before. "Do you have any grain?"

Alana's brows drew together. "Grain?"

He rubbed the area just above his knees. Damn phantom pain. Drove him nuts, but his doctor had told him it was common in both paraplegics and amputees.

"Get a bucketful. Well, not full, but enough that he can hear the corn rattlin' around."

Her face cleared. "Okay, yeah. Sure."

Alana shot off, Trent watching her backside—despite telling himself not to.

"What are you thinking?" Cabe asked.

I'm thinking that is one sexy woman.

"I think the horse needs to learn not all roping boxes are for work." He waved his arm. "Rana, bring him on over here."

"I'll try," Rana said, her voice thick with unshed tears.

"Get off if you have to," he said.

It wasn't something he normally encouraged. It taught the horse that bad behavior meant no human, but this one time wouldn't hurt.

Rana seemed only too happy to get off Scooter's back. The horse's transformation was remarkable. His head instantly dropped, his muscles relaxing—as if he were a balloon and someone let the air out of him. His nostrils still flared as he sucked in breaths, but he was no longer Thunder, Stallion of the Wild.

"I just sent Alana off to get a bucket of grain," he told the teenager when she came up to the rail. "For the next few weeks, I want you to feed your horse out here."

When the girl lifted her brows, Trent noticed she looked a lot like her dad. Hard to believe she'd been paralyzed a few years ago.

"In the arena?" she asked.

"In the roping box. Every morning and every night. Today we're going to get him in the box, with you on him, using grain. Bribe him, if you will. He's going to learn to stand still, and when he does, he'll get a reward."

She nodded.

"I've dealt with this problem in the past." He gave the girl a smile meant to reassure her. "You'll need to take him to some practice pens. Get him off the property. Don't get on him when you're there, just get there early, hang a hay net and leave him."

The girl's tears had faded. "How long should we do it for?"

"At least a couple weeks."

"She has a competition in two weeks," Cabe said.

Trent nodded. "That should give you enough time. Next week, saddle Scooter up and lead him to the box, but don't get on, just feed him."

Cabe was smiling. "Psych him out."

"Exactly." His gaze hooked on Alana, who'd returned with a bucket of corn. "How was he out of the box before he started having problems?"

"I was leading the year-end points," the girl said sadly.

"You will again."

A smile burst upon her face, one that heaped a pile of guilt on him for treating her so poorly. He hated when kids cried, and he would bet he'd made this one cry. Stupid legs. The frustration he felt always there, right beneath the surface, once in a while rearing its ugly head. It made an appearance now, too. If he'd had the use of his damn legs, he would have gotten on the horse and made him get in that box, damn the horse's crazy antics. But he couldn't, and for a moment it was hard to breathe.

"You want me to feed it to him?" Alana asked, and something about the way she stared down at him made Trent wonder if she sensed his frustration. Her gaze had softened, her eyes peering down at him with something resembling pity.

He sucked in a breath. "I'd like Rana to get back on and for you to get in the box and shake that bucket."

She stared at him for a moment, the pitying look slowly fading. "Okay." She nodded, but in such a way that Trent thought she knew how much her pity bothered him. "Got it."

Rana mounted and Scooter's head lifted, the animal trying to turn around while she was still swinging her leg over its back.

"Go ahead and shake the bucket," he told Alana. Scooter didn't appear to notice. The animal was too busy trying to run off with Rana again.

"Scooter, stop it," Rana commanded.

"You might need to bring the grain to him."

Alana, already on the move, swung the bucket. It took a few attempts on Rana's part to get the horse turned around, and a few more shakes of the pail for Scooter to realize that a treat was on hand. His whole attitude changed when he spotted the grain. It was almost comical the way his eyes widened, his nose flaring for a whole different reason this time.

"Careful you don't get run over," Trent cautioned as the horse began to power walk in Alana's direction.

"No kidding." She quickened her pace.

Scooter had a one-track mind, and that mind was now on food. He walked into the box without a problem.

"Just feed him by hand." Trent moved his chair a little so he could see better. Damn it. He hated sitting on the outside.

"Good boy." Rana patted her horse's neck.

"Now walk in and out a few times."

It reminded Trent of a pony ride, Scooter following Alana around as if she was his new best friend—and in his eyes, she probably was.

"Okay. Head back to the box."

In and out the pair went, and when the grain bucket was empty and Alana walked out of the arena, Scooter appeared to have forgotten all about his earlier spastic attack.

"Go ahead and get off him," Trent called. "Give him a big pat."

Rana's smile was every bit as bright as the sun. So was Alana's when she came back to the arena without the blue bucket.

"That was great." She was one of those women who went from pretty to gorgeous when she smiled. "Scooter completely forgot about running out of the box."

"You'd be amazed how food can motivate a horse."

"Thank you." It was Rana who'd spoken. Somehow she'd

managed to scale the fence in record time. "You make me think that maybe we can fix him."

She all but knocked him in the chin when she bent down, her arms wrapping around his middle and pulling him forward a bit. She squeezed him so hard it became hard to breathe.

"Whoa, there."

She drew back. "You're my hero, Trent Anderson."

He couldn't move for a moment.

You could be a hero to someone else.

Alana's words came back to him as, for the second time since he'd arrived, Trent found himself choked up.

"Yeah, well, you say that now, but we still have a lot of work ahead of us."

"Whatever you tell me to do, I'll do." Rana straightened. "I'm not afraid of hard work."

"Good."

He used his hands to push himself back.

And felt a pain in his leg.

He froze. Pain? Impossible. He hadn't felt anything but a nagging ache for months—phantom pain—that was all it was, his doctors had assured him.

"What's wrong?" Alana came forward. "You look like you've seen a ghost."

He rubbed his legs again. "Nothing."

She didn't look as if she believed him. Her eyes had shifted to his legs, following the motion of his hands.

"Just tired, is all."

He turned his chair away and almost gasped. His calf cramped.

Chapter Ten

"Trent, what's wrong?" Alana knelt in front of his chair, her heart banging against her chest when she spotted the look of agony on his face.

"Nothing," he gasped.

"Is it your back? Is it hurting?" She placed a hand on his leg…and he winced.

Winced.

"It's your leg," she said, squatting down so she could get a better look at it. "Your muscles hurt?"

His lips had begun to lose their pinched appearance. "It's my calf. And it's just a phantom pain. I was getting those a lot in the hospital."

She stared at the limb in question. "In the hospital? But not since?"

His eyes flicked to hers in such a way that she knew he'd figured out where she was going with that line of questioning.

"It's nothing." He started to wheel himself away.

When Alana straightened, Cabe's and Rana's eyes were wide, their gazes shifting from Trent to her and then back again. She gave them a look, one that was the nonverbal equivalent of *stay here.*

He was halfway to the barn when she caught up with him. "Trent, wait." He seemed to shove on his wheels even harder. "Trent."

He slowed down, his shoulders slumped in resignation.

When he turned to face her, she could tell he wasn't pleased that she'd followed him.

"What if it's not phantom pain?"

"It is."

"Can I take a look at your legs?"

His shoulders pulled back so fast, it was a wonder he didn't topple over backward. He didn't answer her.

"We can do it right here—"

"No." He turned around again, and Alana realized he was headed for the pathway off the back of the barn. She let him go this time, turning around and walking back to Rana and Cabe.

"You think he's getting better?" Rana's face showed her surprise.

"I think he's been better for a while." She met Cabe's gaze. They both turned and watched as Trent disappeared between the trees.

"He's hiding something and I'm going to find out what."

Cabe and Rana didn't say a word. She drove by them a few minutes later, waving. It had started to cool off, the sun on the verge of sinking behind the mountains, the trunks of pine trees splashed by an orange glow. She didn't rush. She wanted to give Trent plenty of time to arrive, although she knew he wouldn't be glad to see her.

He wasn't.

She crested the small hill as he reached the ramp of his cabin, his chair instantly swiveling in her direction, cowboy hat tipping back as he peered up at her. She gunned the accelerator. He spun toward his cabin.

"Trent," she called, the vehicle picking up speed as it motored down the hill.

He opened the door and disappeared inside.

"Damn."

She didn't let his attitude deter her, though, as she slid to a stop in front of his cabin. This was a make-or-break moment. She knew if she backed away now, she might never get a second chance.

"Trent?" she called, knocking on his front door. She glanced right, trying to spot him through the cabin's picture window, but he'd drawn the drapes. "Trent?"

Frogs sang a noisy chorus from the banks of the river behind her. The orange glow began to fade from the sky, replaced by darker shadows that formed puddles in the deep corners of the porch. She hesitated for a moment before grabbing the handle of the door and pushing.

"What the—"

He still sat in his chair. Still wore his frown like a no-trespassing sign. Still wore his clothes—thankfully—but no hat. That he'd tossed on the couch.

"I'm not taking no for an answer."

"You've got a lot of nerve, lady."

"Take off your pants."

If she hadn't been so perturbed, she might have laughed at the way his eyes widened.

"Excuse me?" His hands found his wheels and slid his chair backward…away from her.

"Take off your pants." She placed her hands on her hips.

"I will not." She saw his chest expand, his dark blond hair mussed, his jaw thrust forward, shoulders so tense she could have bounced pennies off them.

"I need to look at your legs."

He pushed his chair back even more. "Not today."

"Do I need to take your pants off for you?"

"No."

She approached slowly, as if he were a fractious calf in need of doctoring. "I've watched you ride. Both Cabe and I spotted the telltale signs of muscle control as you clung to Baylor's back. You were flexing your legs. Not always, but enough times that I suspect you have something there."

"Impossible."

She took another step. "And if that's the case, then I swear to you, Trent, I will not rest until I have a shot at helping you heal, and the first step I need to take in helping you is examining your legs."

His head flicked up. "Why?" She watched his Adam's apple bob as he swallowed. "Why do you care?"

She closed the distance between them, slowly squatted down by his side. "Because inside that damaged body of yours is the heart of a good man, one that cared enough to help Rana today. That heart might be hidden behind anger and bitterness, but it's there, I know. And that heart is huge, I can tell, and you're going to need it to combat what's going on up here." She tapped her head.

His eyes had begun to shutter like an old building, wooden boards all but crossing the surface of his face. His lips were tight, hands clenching and unclenching.

"So you're saying I have mental issues?"

"No." She leaned closer to him. "I'm saying your accident damaged more than your legs."

She rested a hand on his thigh. Did he feel it? She knew he had some use of his upper thighs, so it wasn't outside the realm of possibility. He peered into her gaze so intently it was hard to notice anything other than the spectacular color of his eyes.

"It's not in my head."

Had he been told that before? Would he resist her now? Was he afraid of what she might find?

"Trent, as your therapist, I'll need to examine your legs sooner or later. Please. Let me have a look at them."

He wanted to refuse. She saw the muscle in his jaw clench with tension. He broke eye contact.

"Fine."

HE COULDN'T BELIEVE he was doing this, Trent thought a few minutes later. Outside his bedroom Alana waited for him to strip out of his clothes—a long, tedious process that could have been helped along by Alana if he'd thought for one moment that he could have remained unaffected by the sight of her unzipping his jeans.

Oh, hell.

He just needed to get this over with. He stripped, pulled himself atop the bed, jerked a blanket over his midsection and gathered the courage to call her into his room. He'd left his legs exposed, but the thought of her touching them…well, thank goodness he'd pulled the blanket over his middle.

"Okay."

His voice sounded hoarse, his heart thudded in his chest, and his whole body was tense as he waited for her to enter. When he felt himself clutch at the brown bedspread, he told himself to relax.

"Hey."

She peeked around the door, her long black hair hanging over her shoulders, a smile on her face. The sun had slipped below the horizon, shrouding his room in darkness, a single lamp by his bed casting light over his form. He'd wanted it that way.

He watched her straighten, and he almost clenched the bedspread again as she came into the room and her blue eyes swept over his form.

I am crippled. She doesn't find me attractive. No woman will ever find me attractive again.

"Oh!"

Her gasp was so soft, yet so sudden he knew she'd seen.

"Oh, Trent."

Scars crisscrossed his legs, the marks looking like sleep wrinkles in some places, deep gouges in others. Across his right thigh was the worst one. A long, angry red spot where they'd had to perform a skin graft to plug the hole the passenger door had left behind.

"I don't feel them. The scars, I mean. It's all numb from the thighs on down."

He could tell she worked hard to put her professional mask back on, though surely she'd seen worse in her career as a therapist.

"Let me feel your muscle tone."

He tensed. She sat down on the bed next to him. That wasn't the worst of it. Oh, no. She would touch him. He didn't want her to touch him. The reason why became instantly apparent when he saw her reach for his leg.

Anticipation shot straight to his groin.

He nearly groaned. The one spot that still worked perfectly—it came to life. He tried to focus on other things, on the unique color of her hair. On the way that hair fell across her shoulder. Or how it hugged her face—

He moaned.

"I haven't even touched you yet."

His eyes snapped open. When had he closed them?

"I have another cramp," he lied.

"Where?"

"Right below my hip, but it's okay now."

She nodded. Her fingers skated over his naked flesh, not that he felt anything. Still, watching her do that…

"I'm going to press on you." She met his gaze briefly. "Tell me what you feel."

Nothing.

He just imagined the soft drag of her fingers. Fantasized that his lower leg tingled from her touch. Suddenly he wished with every fiber of his being that she was touching him for a different reason. Her hand moved slowly up his leg, paused for a moment where he'd been rubbing his knee earlier, but he couldn't feel it. He couldn't feel anything.

"Lots of scar tissue." She leaned back. "Let me take a look at the other one."

He watched her lean forward again, watched her fingers skim and then press against his thigh, rubbing gently, then moving downward, pressing harder and harder—

"That's enough." His voice sounded gritty even to his own ears.

"Do you feel something?" she asked, her eyes snapping to his.

"No," he all but shouted. "I don't." He tried to throw the covers over his limbs.

She wouldn't let him. "I'm not through yet."

"You saw what you came to see."

"No, actually. I want to do an assessment. Move your legs around a bit."

"Forget it." He pushed himself up against the headboard. "You don't need to look at my legs in order to see how messed up they are."

"You're not messed up." She touched his calf, not that he could feel it. "You still have muscle tone."

He huffed. "You call that muscle?"

"Compared to what you had, sure, it's not much, but the fact is, Trent, there's very little atrophy."

He'd heard that before, and he knew where she was going with it. "That's because of the therapy."

Her eyes were amazing to look at, even in the dusky half-light. So blue, yet with a ring of green around them.

"Then obviously that therapy is working."

He pushed himself up against his headboard. "You call this working?" He motioned to his legs. "Not being able to move them. Not being able to feel. Not being able to do anything but roll myself around in a stupid wheelchair."

She drew back a bit, her whole face softening. "I know it's not much." She shook her head a bit. "I'm so sorry, Trent. This whole thing has obviously been tough on you."

No. Not pity. He could take anything from her but pity. "If you've seen what you wanted to see, you can go now." He was still hard, though, damn it. Didn't his body know that she would never find a broken-up old cowboy attractive?

"Were you conscious after the wreck?"

It was as if she'd smacked him. As if each word stabbed at his heart.

POW!

"I don't want to talk about it."

An explosion, that was what it'd sounded like when their

car had been struck head-on. A grenade going off right in his face. One minute driving. The next…not. Dustin's cries. His own moans of agony. His legs. God, he'd thought he'd lost his legs, and in a way, he had.

"But we *should* talk about it."

"I'm tired now. Need rest."

"How long were you there waiting for help to come?"

Why would she not leave him alone? Nobody had dared to ask him such questions before. "I told you, I don't want to talk about it."

"Five minutes? Ten? Twenty?"

"Stop." She'd completely killed the buzz of attraction he'd felt earlier. He should be grateful for that, he told himself, and yet, how long had it been since he'd felt something, anything other than lingering physical pain?

"You *were* conscious, weren't you?"

"I don't remember!"

He hadn't meant to yell, felt bad afterward. She had leaned away from him again, peering down at him from the edge of the bed. And all of a sudden she looked sad.

"I wasn't in the wreck that killed Kim and Braden." She blinked a few times, her lips pressing together for a moment as she thought back to the day that was her own personal cross to bear. "I'd stayed home to look after the ranch. Cabe, though…" She shook her head, met his gaze again. "Cabe saw the whole thing. He was following behind in his truck, towing the horses home. The air-conditioning was out in the truck, and Kim couldn't stand the heat, so she and Rana rode with Braden. Cabe said one minute the car was on the road and the next it wasn't. It happened that fast." She snapped her fingers. "By the time he got the rig stopped, he was already past them, so he ran back, but when he caught sight of the car, and then heard Rana's screams—"

She didn't have to finish the sentence.

He knew. He'd been there.

He'd known Dustin was dead when the moans of pain had

stopped. Hours. That's how long it felt, but it hadn't been hours. Someone had tried opening his door almost right away, but it'd been wedged shut. Wedged? Hell. Crumpled. Crushed. Like his legs. Like Dustin against the steering wheel. Punctured lung. Internal bleeding. It had killed him almost instantly, they'd said, but *not* instantly. He'd had to sit there, listening as his best friend's cries of pain had slowly…

"He said he knew Braden and Kim were dead because he couldn't hear them, and that hearing Rana's cries, realizing she was trapped and that he couldn't get her, was the worst feeling of his life." She shook her head again, the rims of her eyes turning red with unshed tears. "I can only imagine what he saw when they started tearing the car apart. He's never told me, and I've never asked, but the point is, Trent, he *does* talk about it. It's important that you do, too. You can't bottle it up inside. It's not good for you. It can lead to other…problems."

He didn't bottle it up. He couldn't. Oh, no. His subconscious made him remember. At least once a week he relived the moment of turning to his left, of seeing Dustin there, eyes glazed with pain, trapped as he was, moaning, and then those eyes closing and he knew, he'd just known—

"Please leave."

Tears had started to fall. He didn't want her seeing them.

"Not before I finish what I have to say." She fumbled, and then found his hand, clutching it. Her flesh was warm, her fingers soft. "The police labeled it distracted driving, and I know that's what it was because I had sent Braden a text. Right after they left the rodeo grounds. That's when it happened. So it was my fault." She squeezed his hand harder, wiped at her *own* eyes with her other hand. "Cabe says it's not, but I wanted Braden to hurry home, so I told him that in a text, only he never made it back to the ranch because when he glanced to read what I had written…"

He'd wrecked.

Trent felt the power of her words right in his gut. He knew

exactly how she felt. He'd been in such a hurry to leave the rodeo grounds, but if they'd just waited five more minutes…

"So I know a little something about survivor's guilt." She wiped at her eyes with both hands this time. "I know how it can weigh on you. The effects it can have on your mind. But you can't let it ruin your life, Trent. Your doctors all say you should have the ability to walk—"

"No—"

"Shh." She lifted a hand. "Don't say anything. I want you to think about this. I want you to understand that your problem is probably up here." She tapped her head. "And we're going to fix it."

He didn't say anything.

She stood up then, stared down at him. "You just need to believe."

"You'll never be able to fix me. I can't be fixed." But was he talking about his spinal injury, or something else? Shit, he didn't know.

"We'll see about that."

Chapter Eleven

"What are you doing?"

Alana turned away from the truck she'd just finished stocking with snacks and drinks. It'd been a long night, one where she'd done a lot of thinking. When the day had dawned beautiful and bright, she took it as a sign to go through with the plan she'd hatched last evening, one that had involved making a few phone calls.

"I'm going on a road trip." She turned to find Cabe on the front porch, a look of curiosity mixed with surprise on his face.

"By yourself?" He slowly descended the porch, the spurs he wore tapping the wood and punctuating each step with a ching-ching-ching.

"No." She smiled, glanced up at the blue sky above them. It had truly dawned a glorious day, warm, the scent of wild daisies in the air. "With Trent."

Beneath his cowboy hat, Cabe's brows shot up. "Does Trent know this?"

Alana's determination faded a bit. She'd left him alone all morning. "No. Not yet."

Cabe's soft laugh rang out. He stopped in front of her, flat cowboy hat tipped low, denim shirt darker than the sky. "Why am I not surprised?"

She didn't answer, just closed the back door of the crew cab. Though it was early afternoon and still cool outside, she'd started to sweat.

Maybe you're sweating at the thought of being cooped up in a car with Trent for two hours?

And maybe she was, but, damn it, she needed to do something to get through to him. So she'd come up with a plan. More of an idea, really. If she couldn't talk some sense into him, maybe someone else could.

"Did you get a look at his legs last night?"

She tucked her hands in her pocket. "I did. And they were fine. I honestly think his problem is up here." She tapped her head. "I tried to talk to him about it, but I couldn't get him to open up about the accident at all. He shut down."

"So where are you taking him?"

"It's a surprise."

This time Cabe's brows nearly touched the brim of his hat. "Where?" he repeated.

"I'd rather not say because if I tell you, you'd probably try and talk me out of it."

He laughed again. "The poor guy has no idea how determined you can be."

"I know." She glanced at her watch. "We need to get going if we're going to make it on time."

She left him standing by the road, her stomach rolling as she headed toward Trent's cabin. Of course, this late in the day, he could be anywhere. Maybe strolling around in his wheelchair. Or petting horses somewhere on the property, but she suspected he wasn't. She suspected he'd holed himself up in his residence like a wounded bear.

And he had.

"What?" was the greeting she received when she knocked on the door.

"Thought you might like to get out for a bit." She could smell the lingering remains of bacon and eggs, though he hadn't opened the door. "Trent?"

Silence.

She tried the handle, gently, so he wouldn't hear. Locked. Damn it.

She knocked again, her knuckles stinging she tapped so hard. "Come on, Trent. Open up."

No answer. Well, there was more than one way to skin a cat. Though she knew he wouldn't like it, she still went to the rock near the edge of the front walkway, lifted it and removed a key from beneath it.

"Nothing ventured, nothing gained," she told herself as she straightened. Before she could think better of it, she slid the key home, turned the knob. The door opened with barely a whisper.

"What the—"

He sat in the middle of the hall, out of range of the front window, near the entrance to his bedroom. And thank goodness he was dressed, though the black shirt he wore made him appear menacing. Or maybe it was the daggers he tossed at her with his eyes.

"Thought you'd like to go for a ride."

She motioned behind her, to the truck parked in front of his place, sunlight arcing across its black surface and turning it silver in places.

"No." He rolled his chair back, toward his bedroom. She moved quickly, blocking him. Man, their heart-to-heart last evening must have really hit a nerve.

"Let me rephrase that." She smiled down at him, a part of her grateful he wore his jeans, too, because touching him last night had been an exercise in self-control. If he only knew how hard it'd been to keep her fingers from lingering on his legs. How ridiculously bizarre her thoughts had been—like what he might do if she bent down and kissed—

"We're going on a field trip," she announced brightly, determined to keep her mind on business. Sheesh, she was his therapist after all.

"Excuse me?"

"I'm your therapist. You have to listen to me." She hastily tacked on, "Your mother told you so."

He glared. She knew she fought a losing battle, so she tried a different tactic. "Come on." She gave him a grin meant to match the sunshine outside. "Don't you want to get out of here for a little bit? It's such a nice day."

He didn't answer.

She took a step closer to him. "I promise not to talk to you about the wreck, if that's what's holding you back. Or your injuries. Or anything else that might make you uncomfortable." She pleaded with her eyes. "Please?"

He wanted to say no, she could tell.

"With sugar on top," she added.

His lips unfurled from their frown. "Where did you want to go?"

"It's a surprise," she said brightly.

"I hate surprises."

Her smiled slipped a notch. She could almost guarantee he wouldn't like this one, either.

"Come on. We'll be back before you know it."

Okay, so that was a small lie, but she knew he wouldn't agree if she told him the truth, so she fudged it a bit.

"Please," she said again.

He caught her eye. In that instant she got a glimpse of the man she'd seen out at the arena. The one who'd helped Rana. The one who didn't like to disappoint people. She liked that man.

"When will we be back?"

"Late afternoon." As in, *really* late afternoon. Okay, maybe even this evening, but she couldn't tell him that because then he'd know. Heck, he might even put it together before they reached their destination.

"I don't really want to go anywhere."

"Okay. No problem. I'll just call your mom and tell her you're refusing to cooperate again."

"No." He frowned. "Fine. I'll go."

She almost jumped in glee even as the guilt made it hard to look him in the eye. She wouldn't have called his mother. "Great."

She didn't ask if she could help him into her truck. Frankly, she had no idea if he could manage it on his own, but he did, opening the door then using his arms to hoist himself up… and using his legs, too, to prop himself up. He might not have noticed it himself, but she caught the way he momentarily leaned on them. Uh-huh, just as she thought. He really *could* use them…if he wanted.

Once he was inside, she stashed his chair in the crew cab of the truck and they were off, Cabe and Rena waving from the front porch as they drove by, Alana smiling back. Trent didn't so much as glance in their direction. Now that he'd agreed to go, she wondered if he regretted his decision.

"I'm really glad you agreed to go," she said after reaching the end of the long driveway with still no words being exchanged. "You'll see, it's a really pretty drive."

He nodded once. As a response, she supposed it would do, but to fill the silence, she turned on the radio. The familiar sound of "Life is a Highway" rang through the cab.

"I actually like the Chris LeDoux cover of this song better than the Rascal Flatts version."

When she glanced over at him, his expression clearly said, *yeah, okay.*

"I love Chris LeDoux songs. I hear his concerts were something else."

A nod again, then a small "Yeah."

Well, at least they'd progressed to a word now. That was something.

"What an amazing life. Rodeo cowboy, world champion, Garth Brooks mentioning him in that song and then, suddenly, world fame. Did you know he sold nearly a quarter of a million albums out of the trunk of his car, all of them recorded in his dad's basement?"

"Do you really blame yourself for Braden's death?"

She nearly swerved. The question, coming as it did out of the blue, was a shock.

"I did." She swallowed hard. "It took me a few months to

realize Braden didn't have to do what he did, he didn't have to glance down at his phone. He could have ignored me."

"But he didn't."

Was he trying to make her feel uncomfortable? Was that his plan? Revenge for threatening to call his mother? "He didn't, and that was his choice."

He went back to staring out the passenger window. Time to ask him a hard-hitting question then, she thought.

"Do you honestly think Dustin would be angry that you survived the wreck and he didn't?"

That got his attention. He no longer stared outside the window.

"Think about it, Trent, because I'm sure somewhere in that cranium of yours is a sense of guilt that you're too proud to admit you have. Never mind the physical trauma you've been through, my point is you don't survive a wreck where your best friend died without feeling *something*."

His head tipped away. "Was psychotherapy part of your training?"

He'd meant the words sarcastically, but she didn't care. "I majored in sports medicine, but I took psychology classes, too, mostly because I wanted to be able to help athletes through the mental game of making a comeback once they'd been rehabilitated."

His jaw muscle ticked, as if he was clenching his teeth, but he might be tuning her out, too. He wore no hat today, but he still managed to appear the consummate cowboy with his five-o'clock shadow and square chin. He'd fit right in at a roping or a branding. Well, aside from the wheelchair.

"Are you hearing what I have to say? You don't have to be ashamed of yourself. Or your injuries. Let go of your shame. Be proud that you're a survivor."

She didn't think he would answer, but he did. "Nothing to be proud of. I lived. Dustin didn't."

"Don't waste that life, then."

"I don't plan to."

At last. A conversation of sorts.

"You'd make a hell of a coach. I'm sure one of the inter-collegiate rodeo teams would love to have you."

"Do you compete?"

The question took her by surprise. "You mean on the rodeo circuit?" She shook her head. "I was never much into rodeo. I met Braden in high school. If it wasn't for him, I wouldn't know a pigging string from a barrier."

That wasn't exactly true. It was impossible to grow up in northern California without being aware of cowboys and rodeo, but neither had been her thing. She'd been the science geek. He'd been the high school rodeo star. They'd met in P.E. The rest had been history, until... She shook the thought away.

If wishes were horses, beggars would ride.

"Do you even like rodeos?"

"I like them." She tucked a stray wisp of hair behind her ear. "I just don't like the lifestyle. All those performances. Wondering when you'll get your next paycheck. So many days on the road."

Finally, he held her gaze. "So, it's safe to say you wouldn't have been the type to throw yourself at me back when I was world champion."

What was it about him that could catapult her into an instant bout of self-awareness? Damn it.

"You're *still* a world champion." She flipped on her blinkers and prepared to turn onto the main highway. "And, no, I'm not, nor have I ever been, a buckle bunny." She glanced around to make sure the road was clear. "What about you? Got a girlfriend?"

She peeked at him in time to see him smirk. "Got a friend. She's a girl."

"How long have you known her?"

"Since college."

"You went to college?"

He nodded, but only a small one. "Majored in communications."

"Ah." She smiled in his direction. "The truth comes out. You secretly want to be a broadcaster."

"No. I received a scholarship and when it came time to declare a major, I chose something that would allow me to meet pretty girls."

She laughed. "Seriously?"

"Seriously."

They settled into an easy conversation then. As they drove through pine-studded hills and then, later, through a desert valley, she learned his "friend who was a girl" owned a business that she'd just sold, and that she was making a bid for the National Finals Rodeo next year in barrel racing. And that his mother was his best friend. And that before his wreck, he'd been thinking about retiring to his ranch in Colorado, only he'd wanted to win one more championship, had been poised to do exactly that…before.

She told him about her dream of working for a football team. It all sounded silly now, almost childish. She no longer watched pro ball every weekend. And these days she couldn't imagine a life away from the ranch, but that's what her goal had been, back when she was nineteen. Six years and the death of the man she'd been slated to marry sure could change things.

"Just where the heck are you taking me?"

Oops.

She'd managed to forget their destination, at least for a little while.

"You'll see," she said evasively.

"In another half hour we'll be in…"

She knew what he'd been about to say: Reno.

And then he straightened, his face going slack for a moment before he shot her a look that made her wince.

"Where. Are. You. Taking. Me?" His words were sharp—like gunfire.

But he'd figured it out, even though she'd purposely tried to keep him distracted, and herself, if she was honest.

"Surprise," she said. "I thought you might like to see some of your old friends."

His face had gone ashen, his lips from relaxed to taut.

"Turn the heck around."

Her stomach flipped again. "Too late."

Chapter Twelve

He would have jumped from the truck, except he couldn't. No matter how much he demanded she turn around, she ignored him.

"I don't have tickets yet," she said as they crested a small hill, houses and industrial buildings sprawled out to the left of the freeway, barren brown mountains to the right. "I figured we could purchase them at the door."

"You can't make me go in." Anger made it difficult to form words for a moment. "I won't."

"Nonsense."

He turned on her before he could think better of it. "What the hell is your problem?" He didn't wait for an answer. "Don't you get it? I don't want anything to do with the sport of rodeo. Not anymore."

"You'll change your mind."

Fifteen minutes later, the massive Livestock Event Center loomed in the distance. A banner stretched across the roadway, one that read Reno Rodeo: Richest Rodeo in the West and one he'd seen numerous times over the years.

He groaned inwardly.

"Crowded for being so early," she muttered to herself as she navigated traffic. "I thought the rodeo didn't start for a couple of hours yet."

"I warn you. I'm not leaving this truck."

"Yes, you are."

Never, *ever,* had he felt so impotent. And so angry. Not since he'd woken up from a medically induced coma and discovered he was paralyzed. Not since Saedra had told him his worst fear had come true: Dustin was dead. Not since he'd seen his bid for another world championship come to a screeching, grinding halt.

"You can't make me do something against my will."

He knew he sounded like a petulant child. God, that was all he sounded like lately. But he flat-out refused to do her bidding.

As it turned out, he had little choice.

She parked in the spectator area, but the lot was butted up next to competitor parking, and some familiar faces were less than twenty feet away. He tried to scrunch down in his seat because the last thing he wanted or needed was for someone to recognize him. As she pulled into a spot, he could plainly see the men and women riding horses, carrying rigging bags or walking back to their trailers. Damn it. Why hadn't he worn a cowboy hat? At least then he could have shielded his face with the brim of his hat.

"I'll get your chair."

"No—"

She was out of the truck before he could say another word, reappearing again on the other side, the maroon long-sleeved T-shirt she wore hugging her every curve. It had a black scroll-like design across the front, one that seemed to accentuate her chest, and Trent wondered if she'd worn the thing on purpose. Coupled with her jeans she looked entirely too sexy for his peace of mind.

"Okay. Here we go." She quickly removed and then opened his chair. When she pulled on his door next, he didn't move.

"I told you, I'm not getting out."

"Then we're going to have a problem." She swiped a strand of hair off her face, the long tresses so black they almost looked blue in the afternoon light.

"Leave me here."

"No. Your friends wouldn't like that."

It took a moment for her words to penetrate, and then in an instant he gleaned her plan. Still, he asked, "What friends?"

She smiled. "The ones who expect to see you today." Though maybe that grin was tinged with guilt. "I called your mom this morning. She, in turn, called some of your rodeo buddies." Alana increased the brightness of her smile. "Quite a few of them are here already, apparently all anxious to see you. I'm to take you inside no later than five."

He was going to kill his mother.

"I guess it's been a while since your friends have seen you."

Not since the hospital. Sure, they'd called. He'd ignored them.

"Come on." She patted the chair. "I don't want to be late. I guess one or two of them are competing tonight."

In the distance, he could hear screams coming from the carnival rides out front. His own screams echoed inside his head.

"By the way, your mom said if you give me any trouble, I'm to call some of your friends and tell them to come and get you."

Son of a—

"But I'd really hate to do that." She stuffed her hand in her pocket, withdrawing a black cell phone. "Still, I have all their numbers programmed…"

"Fine."

He had no choice. She'd known that. Just like she'd known earlier that threatening to call his mother would get him to do her bidding. This whole thing had been a setup.

"Good." She tucked her phone back in her pocket, with good reason. Once his friends realized he was in Reno, they'd hunt him down. He knew it and she knew it, too. Damn it.

She patted his chair as if he were a damn five-year-old. He twisted in his seat, pushed himself toward the edge with the help of a handle near the front door. His legs unfolded all on their own as Alana placed the chair beneath him.

"All set?" she asked when he was settled.

He didn't answer.

"You'll have to point out your friends, although I suppose

they'll recognize you all on their own. We're right on time, so they should be on the lookout. I think they have a welcome-back party scheduled."

She wheeled him toward the competitors' entrance. Behind him, he could hear cows mooing, people laughing, and more vehicles arriving.

In all too short a time, he heard a woman call out, "Trent!" and his head jerked up. "That you?"

Saedra.

Despite his dread, his spirits lifted. "What the hell are you doing here?"

Her grin was as bright as the white horse trailers around them. "A bunch of the guys chartered a flight for this morning. They gave me a ride."

"Why, as I live and breathe," someone else said. "If it ain't Trent Anderson."

Buster Stone, one of his closest rodeo friends, came from his right, a wide smile on the cowboy's face, one emphasized by a handlebar mustache that stuck out like cat whiskers. The rodeo announcer looked tickled pink, and despite his anger, Trent found himself smiling back.

"It *is* Trent," another man said, one of his fellow rough-stock riders, a beefy cowboy with a black hat, who came forward and held out his hand. Trent took it.

Before he knew it, he had a crowd around him, old friends and some new coming at him from all directions, although it was Saedra he was most happy to see. Her long blond hair fell nearly to his waist when she bent down and hugged him, the scent of her was so familiar and so very dear to him that he held her for a second longer than necessary.

"I was worried you might not come," she said for his ears alone.

"I wasn't told we *were* coming."

As she straightened away from him, Saedra's eyes shifted to Alana. "I think I'm going to like this girl."

"Move over!"

Trent froze.

"By God, when I heard the rumors, I couldn't believe they were true."

Mac McKenzie barreled through the crowd, nearly knocking Buster on his ass in his hurry to reach him. "Trent Anderson, where the hell have you been?"

Hiding.

"Trying to get well."

His former roping partner damn near jerked him from the chair, and when he drew back, Trent could have sworn he saw tears in his eyes.

"Damn you, Trent Anderson, it's good to see you." He clapped him on the shoulder.

He locked eyes with Alana, startled to admit his anger had completely vaporized because, yes…it was good to be back.

THEY TOOK HIM to a horse trailer with living quarters in the front, someone having hung up a sign that said Welcome Back, Trent across the front of its white surface. Alana smiled when she saw it, happy that she'd gotten him to their destination with a minimum of fuss.

"I can't believe you didn't tell him you were coming here."

Trent's "friend who was a girl" smiled at her, the crowd that greeted them at the gate following in their wake. One of them pushed Trent, although she was certain Trent wasn't happy about that. Still, he bore it well. He was cautiously excited, she noted. No longer miserable, but still a little anxious.

"I knew if I told him what I wanted to do, he wouldn't come."

She glanced back at Saedra just in time to see the side of her mouth tip up. "That's for sure."

She was beautiful, this friend of his. Long, straight blond hair. Blue, blue eyes. And a wide mouth with plump lips that would have been the pride of a plastic surgeon if they'd been fake, although Alana suspected they were completely natural.

She didn't think Saedra was the type of woman who would surgically alter herself.

"I'm glad you made it."

"Me, too." Alana sighed. "The man's been a real pill."

Saedra nodded in commiseration. "You should have seen him before he left. His mom was ready to disown him."

A horse galloped between them and a neighboring trailer, and the parking area where they stood was packed with all types of rigs. In the distance, Alana could hear people laughing and screaming on the rides out in front of the arena. The smell of corn dogs reached them all the way out here.

"He called me the other day, you know," Saedra said. "I think he was hoping I'd tell him to come home."

Were they more than just friends? Alana wondered. By "home," did she mean a home she shared with Trent? Alana searched Saedra's eyes, but she could see no evidence of anything more than curiosity. Of course, the sun was behind them, so the woman's face was partly in shadow.

Taking a deep breath, she uttered the words she hadn't wanted to say to her over the phone. "I don't see why he's not walking."

Saedra froze. "Really?"

Alana crossed her arms. "He has very little atrophy, Saedra, certainly not as much as I would expect, given his disability." She took a deep breath. Friend or girlfriend, the woman might prove a valuable ally in helping Trent. "I think he has PTSD."

The blonde's brows shot up. "Post-traumatic stress disorder?"

"It can do funny things, like make you believe you're paralyzed when you're really not."

They both turned back to Trent. Lord help her, he was actually smiling at something someone said. A relaxed smile. A happy smile, the grin completely transforming his face. He was pleased to be among his friends.

From his right, a scantily clad brunette approached the group, and if her skintight white T-shirt wasn't a dead giveaway as to her intentions, the Daisy Duke shorts and cowboy boots would have sealed the deal.

Oh, great.

If ever she needed a reminder of why she shouldn't, wouldn't, think of this man as more than a patient, there it was. One day he would walk again. More than likely he would rejoin the rodeo circuit, oh, not as a rough-stock rider, but certainly in some other capacity. She wanted no part of rodeo life and the buckle bunnies that went along with it.

"Will he get over it?" Saedra asked.

Alana forced her gaze away from the skimpily clad woman. "With some help."

But she was fascinated. Alana watched as all the men in Trent's group eyed the woman up and down—all except Trent. His gaze connected with hers instead, and good golly, Miss Molly, he smiled at her this time. Alana had to look away because that grin did things that it really shouldn't.

"What can I do to help?" Saedra asked.

Alana took a deep breath and forced herself to concentrate. "Encourage him to listen to me. Tell him not to think of me as the enemy, but an ally. Above all, he needs to do the exercises I prescribe. That should do it for starters."

"Got it."

She glanced at the woman in the skimpy outfit again. She completely ignored Trent. Man in Wheelchair clearly wasn't her thing. Alana wondered what she would do if she found out who Trent was. Would it make a difference? Probably not. Some women couldn't see past the chair.

"Are you going to stay for the rodeo performance?" Saedra asked.

"That's up to Trent."

Saedra touched her arm. Alana quickly turned. There was kindness in the woman's gaze, kindness and friendliness. Alana realized she could like this woman—a lot.

"Thank you—" she squeezed her arm "—for everything you're doing."

"It's my pleasure."

They both turned back to the man they so badly wanted to help. A year ago, this would have been his world, Alana thought. He would have been the one fending off the advances of the little brunette. He would have been the one breaking away less than an hour later to prep for competition. Instead he had to watch as, one by one, his buddies walked away, only Buster hanging behind.

"Almost time to get the show on the road," Buster said, glancing at his watch. "Why don't you ride with me, Trent? I gotta drive one of the sponsor trucks into the middle of the ring. You know the drill. Boring as hell. Could use some company."

"Nah. I'm sure Alana wants to get going."

"Go ahead." She made a shooing motion. "Saedra and I can hang out here."

"Sure would like a copilot," Buster added.

"It's okay—"

"Trent, don't be an ass," Saedra called. "Buster hasn't seen you in forever. Hang out with the man."

His need to please once again reared its head. "All right," he said slowly. "As long as Alana doesn't mind me ditching her for a bit.

Alana's heart leaped, although not because of the soft smile he'd just given her. No. She'd just been struck by an idea. A brilliant idea. A fabulous one. If Trent couldn't be pressured into using his legs by her, maybe a thousand screaming fans…

"Not at all." She forced herself to remain calm. It was a long shot, but it might work. "In fact, I'll walk with Buster back to his truck. It'll be easier if he swings by and picks you up, and I forgot my cell phone." She patted her pocket. "Need to head back to my truck to get it. You and Saedra stay here. Buster can give me a ride back."

"Sounds good to me," Buster said.

She waved to Saedra and Trent, but the moment they were out of earshot, Alana leaned close to the rodeo announcer. "Buster. I have a favor to ask."

The cowboy's silver brows lifted, his mustache bobbing with a twitch of his mouth.

"A really *huge* favor, and it involves Trent...."

Chapter Thirteen

He hadn't been inside a rodeo arena since his accident, and to be honest, Trent wasn't certain he wanted to be in one now.

"Here we go," Buster said as someone opened the gate to the big arena. "I was thinking I could introduce you to the crowd."

Trent shot upward. "No." He shook his head. "You don't need to do that."

"What do you mean I don't need to do that? You're a big star, Trent. People be glad to see you."

Trent released a breath. People didn't want to see him. Not like this. A helpless paraplegic who would only ever enter a rodeo arena in the passenger seat of a truck.

"I'd rather keep to myself."

"Nah," Buster drawled. "Not going to happen."

Before Trent could say another word, Buster was out of the truck and waving to the audience. Trent resisted the urge to slink down in his seat. Ahead of him the massive grandstand looked packed. It was still bright outside, those in front of him in shadow, but those to the left, right and behind him in full sun.

"Good afternoon, rodeo fans!"

Buster's voice rang out, the words clearly audible even inside the cab, though if he said anything else he was drowned out by the sudden roar of the crowd. Trent didn't listen. Too busy trying not to panic. He would *not* get out of the truck. He didn't care how good a friend Buster was, he would stay right here, to hell with the man.

The crowd quieted. Trent caught a few words here and there, but with every step Buster took, steps that brought Buster closer to his side of the truck, the tempo of Trent's heartbeat increased.

"And here he is!" he heard Buster say with a grand wave in his direction. "Multiple-world-champion cowboy Trent Anderson."

Then Trent's door was wrenched open, and if he'd thought the sound of the crowd was deafening before, it was nothing to when audience members spotted him inside.

Dear God in heaven.

"Trent Anderson, how does it feel to be back?"

Buster held the mic toward him. Trent just stared. Buster scooted closer, slapped him on his knee, hard.

And it hurt.

Trent jerked his gaze up.

"Think he's tongue-tied, ladies and gentlemen. Been too long since he's been in front of a crowd. Don't be shy, Trent. Tell us what you've been up to since you were injured."

"Not much," he managed to spit out through lips that'd gone quickly numb. That hadn't been a real pain. It was a phantom pain. Again.

"I hear you've made great progress with your therapy. In fact, I was told by your therapist that she thinks you're ready to try standing on your own."

What?

"How'd you like to see that, ladies and gentlemen? I think we need to see Trent Anderson stand on his own two feet again, don't you?"

Mild applause turned deafening again. Trent stared at his friend in horror. He must have shut off the mic because the next thing he knew, Buster leaned next to him.

"Don't look so panic-stricken. I'll do most of the talking. Come on. Try and stand."

Trent shook his head. He had no idea if the audience could see him, but he didn't care. There was no way he was getting out of the vehicle.

"I think he needs some more encouragement. Come on. You can do better than that."

Buster reached for him as the audience erupted into cheers and calls.

"No."

But his old friend ignored him, just reached inside and tried to tug him along like a cowboy doctoring a cow.

"I said no."

"And I said yes."

Buster jerked him off his seat. Trent had no idea how he managed to stay on his feet, but he did, and despite his best efforts to stay behind, Trent found himself leaning against his old friend.

The crowd went wild.

Buster rocked back. Trent suddenly found his legs beneath him.

"There," Buster said softly.

It was like he'd practiced in therapy, like he'd done with the rope, that useless exercise that he hadn't thought meant a thing. But it *had* helped.

"How about that, ladies and gentlemen?"

Slowly, Buster eased back, shifting more and more of Trent's weight. Trent found himself fishing for the side of the truck with his hands. He found it, glanced at the audience. They clapped and cheered, a few of them close enough that he could spot the happiness on their faces. They were proud of him. Proud of his "try."

Buster stared down at him with pride in his eyes, too.

Like a parent helping a toddler, he slowly eased away. Trent held his breath as he straightened. Legs beneath him. Balance. *Don't lean too far forward. Steady. Careful...*

He stood.

It was only for a split second. Just a fraction of an instant, and Buster was right there when his legs gave out, but he'd done it. He'd stood.

"Great job." Buster guided him to the edge of the door. "What do you think, ladies and gentlemen? Trent Anderson back on his feet again. Isn't that amazing?"

The crowd kept clapping. Buster turned back to him, his smile as wide as the Mississippi. "Can you get back in the truck on your own?"

"I think so."

Buster clapped him on the back, happiness still in his eyes as he turned back to the audience. "Wow. I can't wait to see him back in action, how about you?" More cheers. "Tonight we have more amazing cowboys and cowgirls to watch. We've got the top bronc rider in the world…"

The rest of what Buster said faded away. Using his arms, Trent hoisted himself farther into the truck and then onto the seat. At some point Buster shut the door, the sound of the audience fading, but Trent's mind still reeled.

Had Alana been right?

Could it be all in his head? Was there a chance he could actually walk again? Did he have a shot at returning to his rodeo roots?

Dear God, he sure hoped so.

HEART IN HER THROAT, Alana watched as Buster pulled to a stop in front of the trailer. Saedra had disappeared, or maybe she'd intentionally left them alone for a moment; Alana didn't know.

He'd stood on his own.

"How was that?" Buster asked, clearly exuberant as he made his way to Trent's door.

"Incredible."

She couldn't see Trent. The reflection on the truck's glass created a glare. When Buster opened the door, Alana felt herself inhale for the first time in what seemed like forever.

"And here's our star." Buster swung the door wide. "Before long you won't need this." He reached in the back for Trent's wheelchair, but before Buster could move, Trent slid from the truck. Alana started to rush forward, but Trent used the side of the cab to stabilize himself and she realized he was doing it again, he was trying to stand, the look of concentration on his face giving it away.

"Well, I'll be damned." Buster pushed the chair toward his friend. "Maybe you don't need this after all."

"No." Trent glanced up at her. "I need it."

As if demonstrating his point, Trent sank into the seat, but he didn't allow himself to plop down. No. He guided himself down slowly.

Hope bubbled through her heart.

"I'll catch you after the rodeo then." Buster caught her eye, winked and smiled. Alana smiled back.

When she hooked gazes with Trent again it was to note the expression on his face. Puzzled. Pleased. Perturbed.

"You asked Buster to do that, didn't you?"

In the distance a bronc rider had been let out of the chute, the audience reacting with loud cheers, but for Alana, it wasn't the crowd that filled her ears. She had a hard time hearing anything over the beat of her heart.

"I did."

He shifted, pushing off quickly in her direction. "How did you know it would work?"

She shrugged. "I didn't."

When he stopped in front of her, he didn't say anything. And then he smiled, a grin unlike one she'd ever seen before, one full of optimism and hope and, yes, even gratitude.

"You know—" he stroked his chin "—I'm thinking I might keep going with this therapy thing."

They left right after the rodeo, Alana so buoyed up by their evening that she didn't think she'd be able to sit still for the two-hour drive back home.

"I should have known where we were going when we were in the car for so long," Trent said.

It was dark outside, although not terribly late. The rodeo

had ended at nine, but they'd left before the bull riding, the last event of the evening, after Saedra hugged them tearfully goodbye. Trent's friend would fly home later that night, but she'd promised to call him when she got home.

"I was worried you might figure out where we were going when you saw the road signs."

She glanced over at him, thinking that he seemed completely different from the man who'd first arrived at New Horizons Ranch. More relaxed. At ease. Happy. "But once I had you in the truck, I knew there'd be nothing you could do. We were going to the rodeo whether you wanted to or not."

She saw him shake his head ruefully. "Did you call Buster and ask for his help?"

She took her eyes off the road long enough to smile. "No. I came up with that on the spot."

"And if I'd fallen on my face?"

"Buster wouldn't let that happen."

He was quiet for a moment. "You're right. He wouldn't have. Buster is a good friend."

They were out on the main highway. Alana forced herself to focus as they made their way out of town. She concentrated so hard perhaps that's why she said, "And Saedra? Is she really just a friend?"

Good Lord, where had that come from?

Out of the corner of her eye, she saw Trent glance at her sharply. "Would it matter if she wasn't?"

How had it happened? How had things gone from simple to complex in a heart-pounding moment?

"Of course it wouldn't matter." She swallowed. Hard. "I was just curious."

Liar!

Because it did matter. She'd watched him this evening, observed him with his friends and also the rodeo fans who'd come up to him afterward. Always gracious. Always kind. He'd accepted the congratulations of perfect strangers with a smile and a handshake that'd made her oddly proud. In just a week she'd given him the confidence to try to stand on his own two feet, and now she could see the gratitude in his eyes and it made her feel…warm.

"She's a friend."

A sigh of relief rushed past her lips, though she told herself it didn't matter if he was in a relationship or not. Trent would only be a part of her life for an instant, a brief moment, that was all. She had her life at the ranch, her career, Rana to take care of. It was madness, pure and utter madness, to consider something more, something that made her squirm just thinking about it, that had her heart speeding as fast as the truck she drove.

She didn't say anything for the rest of the drive, mostly because she was afraid he'd see right through the lie of her not being interested. At one point she figured he'd fallen asleep, his even breaths and closed eyes causing her to take her own eyes off the road more than once. He was so handsome with his face softened by sleep, his hair mussed, his five-o'clock shadow more like a ten-o'clock shadow. Alana shivered as she wondered what it would feel like to have his chin graze her breast….

Stop.

She'd never been so grateful to arrive back at New Horizons in her life, though a quick glance at Trent revealed he wasn't moving. The day must have been exhausting for him, both physically and emotionally, not to mention all their hard work up until now. When she turned the truck off in front of his cabin, he never stirred.

"Trent?"

He didn't move.

"Trent, we're here."

He mumbled something. She slipped out of the vehicle, gently opening the passenger-side door, although why she tried to keep it quiet she had no idea. He needed to wake up. He couldn't spend the night out in her car.

"Trent, I need you to wake up." She nudged him, her hand

resting on his forearm longer than it needed to be. He had soft skin. She remembered that from her examination of his legs, remembered, too, how touching him had made her feel.

Son of a—

Okay. In for a penny, in for a pound, she thought, opening the back and pulling out his chair. Once she had it set up, she nudged him even harder, pausing for a moment to enjoy the warmth of his arm and the way he smelled.

Alana!

"Come on, Trent."

A part of him must have understood, because he leaned toward her as if asking for her help to get out of the truck. When she glanced up, it was to note their heads were inches apart, and that his breath wafted over her face and that she liked, no, *loved* the smell of him. Okay, so maybe not loved. Maybe just deeply appreciated—

His eyes snapped open.

She froze.

"Are we here?"

Still half-asleep. Thank God. Maybe he hadn't noticed her gawking at him.

"Back home. Come on." She urged him out of the truck. He complied, though they almost fell to the ground together, Alana gasping as the full-frontal feel of him singed itself on her mind.

Oh, dear.

He swung out of her arms and into his chair in less than a second. Alana sighed in relief. She just wanted to get him into his cabin so she could go to her own apartment and take a cold shower. The man did it for her, no doubt about it, he always had. Since the moment she'd first met him.

"Here we go," Alana said.

His head tipped back.

"Really?" she asked when she noticed his eyes were still closed. "How in the hell can you still be asleep?"

No answer.

She released a huff of frustration. Here she was, nearly

combusting in her pants thanks to her own silly, physical attraction, and the man was out cold, completely oblivious to the effect he had on her.

She pushed him toward his cabin, pausing only for a moment to retrieve the key, then heading for the front door. Maybe she should leave him in his chair out on the porch. No. In the family room. She couldn't possibly lift him onto bed. And removing his clothes? Hah. That she wouldn't do.

But once she got him inside, she worried that he might tip forward, out of his chair, maybe hit his head. Then what? With a sigh of resignation, she headed for his bedroom, switching on the light, stopping near the edge of his bed.

Now what?

"Trent?" She slipped past his chair, peered down at him. "Come on, Trent. Time for bed."

His head was tilted to the side and, gosh darn it all, he looked so adorable, like a sleeping little boy. Though she told herself not to, she reached out and smoothed his hair, marveling at how soft it was. Then she did something else, something she knew she shouldn't do, but that she was helpless to stop herself from doing. She slid her hand down the side of his face, her fingers grazing the stubble on his cheek, her nails finding the line of his jaw and the ever-present razor stubble.

Good Lord, she loved that razor stubble.

You're sick, her subconscious pronounced.

Maybe so, but she still leaned down next to him, still found herself closing the distance between the two of them, her mouth six inches, then four, then three, then two inches away.

She kissed him.

She meant it to be a quick peck, a soft joining of their lips that he would never feel, never know about—Eve giving into the temptation of the apple—but once they connected, she found herself tipping her head sideways and then increasing the pressure and then...

His arms wrapped around her.

She screeched.

He pulled her onto his lap. Shocked, Alana froze, their gazes connected.

"Now, *this* is my kind of therapy."

Chapter Fourteen

Her expression was one of mortification. Trent didn't care. He pulled her toward him, closing the distance between them.

"No—"

Oh, yes, he thought right before their lips connected again. Kiss him while she thought he was asleep, would she? Hah. He'd been awake since the moment they'd pulled to a stop outside his cabin.

He let her know instantly this would be no innocent kiss, either. His mouth pressed against hers, harder and then harder still until, at last, she opened, his tongue instantly sliding inside.

She moaned, struggled a little bit, but he didn't let up, so damn thrilled that she found him attractive it was all he could do not to toss her on the bed—not that he could really do that, but still. She tasted good. So damn good.

He grew hard. She must have felt it because she wiggled, but not in protest. No, she squirmed against him in a way that made him realize she really did want him bad—just as he wanted her.

Thank You, Lord.

He swirled his tongue around hers, suckled it, tasting her in a way that could leave no doubt as to what he had in mind, crippled or no.

She wrenched away. "Trent!"

"Help me into bed."

"No."

The bedroom light revealed her startled blue eyes, her flushed cheeks, the crimson of her lips.

"Alana, if you leave me hanging like this I swear I'll learn to walk again just so I can chase you around the ranch."

Her face softened. "Trent, we can't."

His hand slid between them, finding and then cupping her center. "Oh, yes, we can."

She lifted her hips, but the motion had the opposite effect, his fingers pressing against her in such a way that it made her gasp.

"There," he pronounced. "That feels good, doesn't it?"

"Yes," she moaned.

"Then don't tell me no."

"Trent." His name was a sigh on her lips, a cry of soft pleasure that prompted him to cup her again.

She didn't move.

No. She stayed on his lap, her head tilting backward, long hair spilling down around her shoulders, Trent feeling more potent and more powerful than ever. She wanted him. Wanted him bad. His wheelchair didn't bother her. Far from it. She used the armrests as a brace for her hands as he continued to stroke her. And he marveled. She wanted him. No doubt about it.

"Trent," she moaned again.

She would climax soon. He wanted that, but he wanted to do more than stroke her, too. He wanted to taste her and thrust himself inside her and watch her face contort as he brought her pleasure, not with his hand, but with that other part of his body, the one that pulsed and throbbed and ached to be set free.

She found him attractive. He just couldn't get over it.

"Alana, shift your weight." He removed his hand just long enough to help support her. "Here. Lean back against my chest."

Their gazes met. She seemed dazed, had to blink a few times before she became aware of what he asked. He wanted her to open for him, to brace herself with a foot on the ground. She did. He wasted no time unsnapping and then unzipping her jeans, nuzzling her hair as he did so. She smelled so good, but she *felt* even better as his fingers found her slick center.

Her hips shot up.

"That's it," he whispered in her ear. "Let it go."

He stroked. She jerked against him again. He nearly groaned. Every time she moved, she brushed his erection. He delved even deeper, finding her center, dipping his finger inside.

"Oh," he heard her mumble. "Oh, oh…"

He would bring her pleasure, this woman. He might be in a wheelchair. He might not be able to walk…yet—perhaps maybe never—but he could do this. His mouth found her ear. He flicked his tongue inside, swirled it.

"Trent!"

She found her release quickly and, holy hell, it was hot to ride along with her. He might be ready to burst himself. He might crave rolling her onto the bed and thrusting himself inside of her, but this was every bit as wild and crazy and exciting as being inside her.

Slowly, she relaxed, her rear end finding his erection once more and prompting him to gasp.

"What?" She turned to face him, grinding into him once more. "Did I hurt you?"

Her hair was mussed, wild, her eyes soft and satiated, and it turned him on.

"I'm just a little—"

He tried to wiggle in his chair.

She must have felt it then, her mouth forming an O before her eyelids lowered in a way that made him throb all over again.

"You have driven me nuts since the moment we first met," she admitted.

"Ditto."

"But I'd be less than honest if I didn't admit to being wildly attracted to you ever since you got off that bus."

"Good to know."

She smirked.

"Maybe we can do something about this crazy attraction," he said softly.

"Maybe we can."

SHE TOLD HIM TO CLIMB on to the bed because, God help her, she wanted him naked. He wasted no time in doing exactly that, and she helped him undress, all but ripping the buttons off his black shirt. Brazen, lascivious, wanton, she thought, kneeling on the bed, still fully clothed, but completely turned on by him.

What are you doing? her subconscious asked yet again.

Something I shouldn't be doing. Something naughty. Something so wicked, she knew if Cabe found out, he might just fire her. But she would take that risk because tonight she didn't care. Tonight, she wanted to be free. Tonight she wanted to indulge herself in a way she'd never done before.

"You're driving me crazy, looking at me like that."

He leaned against the headboard. Still no overt use of his legs, but that would come…in time.

"If I wasn't so damned messed up, I'd flip you on your back and do things that would make your first orgasm feel like child's play," he said as he shrugged out of his shirt, tugging it out of the waist of his jeans and exposing the abs of steel that always made her mouth water.

"But you're not in charge, are you?"

It gave her a thrilling sense of power to know that, too. She'd never been the kinky kind. Jeez, the last time she'd had sex with Braden she'd—

No.

She would not think about that. Braden was in her past. Tonight was all about Trent.

"Jeans next," she ordered, marveling at how merely thinking the word *orgasm* made her throb all over again. The man was like a sex drug. One whiff and she turned into a nymphomaniac.

"I'll need help."

She shifted, reaching him as he started to slide the fabric

over his hips, revealing boxers beneath, blue ones, the bulge beneath them all too obvious. With a quick tug, she had them halfway down his legs, wincing inwardly when she spotted the scars. She found herself leaning forward and brushing them with her lips. One by one she kissed them, pulling the jeans slowly down, revealing the rest of his legs. She had to pause for a moment. His boots were in the way. She tugged them off, and then his socks, and then, finally, his jeans, leaning back when she was done.

Damn.

He might have scars up and down his legs, but they were overshadowed by the magnificence of his upper body. Months of pulling himself in and out of his chair, cars, his bed, had given him the shoulders of a swimmer, the biceps of a weight lifter and the abs of an underwear model. He had chest hair, but not a lot, just enough to make her want to run her fingers through the light brown whorls. Instead she crawled on her knees to his side, reached for the waistband of his boxers and tugged them down.

"You're going to kill me."

"Can you feel anything?"

"All the way to the tops of my thighs."

She met his gaze, and she admitted she'd never felt so innately feminine in her life, not ever. Not even with Braden.

"Good." She bent and captured him with her mouth before she could think better of it.

"Holy…" The rest of his words turned into a gasp as she wrapped her lips around him.

"I would hate for you to miss out feeling this," she said before taking him in her mouth again.

"Oh, jeez."

She wanted to please him so badly that she glided down the length of him as far as she could go, then drew her lips back up again.

He hissed.

She did it again, then again, over and over again until she

could feel his hips quiver, and his legs, too. Yes, even his legs. She paused for a moment, glanced up at him, but he was too far gone to notice anything. She held him completely in her thrall, her mouth causing his hands to clench the covers beneath him, the muscles across his abdomen rippling with each gasp of pleasure. She knew he was close, wondered if she should take him all the way, but she liked the control.

"Not yet," she said.

His eyes sprang open. "What?"

"I said, not yet." She slid off the bed, slowly lowering the jeans over her hips with a zigzag motion of her hips—stripperlike—but she didn't care. She enjoyed how his eyes burned. How he breathed raggedly. How his hands flexed and then unflexed, as if he wanted to reach out and grab her, but he couldn't. She slowly peeled her top off next, sashaying side to side, then hooking her thumbs through her panties and doing the same thing. By the time she finished the heat in his eyes had gone from white-hot to molten lava.

"You're going to kill me."

She smiled, telling him without words her whole intention. Here was a man who'd been through hell and back—she was about to show him a piece of heaven.

"I don't suppose you have a condom?" she asked, settling on the bed and enjoying the way his eyes ran over her body. She should be mortified and yet for some reason she wasn't. For some reason she liked the way his eyes lingered on her breasts.

What had gotten into her?

"I, ah, I wasn't exactly expecting something like this to happen."

No. Of course not. Most women ignored men in wheelchairs, but how in the heck someone could ignore Trent Anderson, even in a wheelchair, was beyond her.

"But there's nothing to worry about," he added. "I mean, I was fully checked out in the hospital and I—"

"Shh." She'd reached his side, her finger gently swiping his lips. "I trust you."

"What about you?"

"I'll be fine."

She was about to tell him she'd never stopped taking the pill after Braden's death when he suddenly jerked her to him, all thoughts of Braden fading away as he forced her to straddle him. Their centers grazed one another's.

She gasped.

He cupped her butt, pushing her along the length of him, Alana's center so primed for his entry, she moaned at the feel of him against her.

"Like that?" he asked.

"Yes," she hissed. "Oh, yes."

He guided her along the length of him again. She grew impatient. When she tried to move, he wouldn't let her.

"Uh-uh-uh." Their gazes met, his filled with amusement and heat and determination. "Not yet."

"Who's trying to kill who, here?" she groaned.

"That's the point." He gently pushed a strand of hair off her face. "Tit for tat."

He gripped her tighter, only allowing her to move mere inches. Sadist. Oh, but how good it felt, and how deliciously sinful. How exquisitely enthralling to feel him there, close, yet not as close as she wanted. She tipped her head back and moaned. He pressed into her, but only a bit, and only enough that when he withdrew, it was nearly painful.

"Don't do that."

He froze.

"No." She shot him a glare. "I meant stop torturing me."

He smiled, and it was such a wickedly teasing grin that she almost—almost—smiled in response.

"Is this what you want?"

He found her center again, plunging deeper.

"Yes," she cried.

He withdrew, only to thrust even deeper.

"Yes, Trent. Yes," she moaned, so completely lost in the feel of him inside of her that she tipped forward, her head resting against his shoulder. "That's what I want."

Deeper and deeper he went, and higher and higher she climbed, losing herself to everything but the feel of him inside of her, and to something else, too. Something magical and special that made her want to hold him to her, tight, forever.

"Alana!"

His cry was one of release, and it was all she needed to follow him down the same magical, amazing road, one that caused her to cry out his name yet again. He crushed her against him, his big arms wrapping around her midsection so tightly that she lost her breath for a second. He wanted to do more, she could tell. If he had strength in his legs he would have wrapped them around her, maybe flipped her on her back. Instead he held her tight, the scent of him—cedar and cinnamon—filling her nose, his heart lub-lubbing beneath her ear, fast at first and then slowing down in time with her own.

"Thank you."

She lifted her head, looked into his beautiful eyes, the glow in them akin to that of a man who'd been hungry for so long that he couldn't believe he'd finally been allowed to feast.

Still, she asked, "For what?"

"For being you."

She smiled softly. "And here I thought I drove you crazy."

"You *do* drive me crazy." His thumb grazed her cheek gently. "But I needed this right now."

She wanted to ask him if he felt her leg against his own, but she didn't want to spoil the moment, so instead she said, "You might rethink that tomorrow." She rested her head against his chest again. "I plan on working you into a sweat."

His chest rumbled against her ear. She realized an instant later that he laughed. "As long as we work up a sweat doing this, I won't mind at all."

She peered up at him again. "You know that's not what I meant."

His face grew serious. "I know."

She moved her foot, brushing it across his calf, hoping to see a spark of recognition. She saw nothing.

"It's not going to be fun," she said.

There was limited light in the room, the lamp to his left casting a shadow over his face. Perhaps that was why his eyes appeared to grow dark for a moment.

"I know."

She hoped so because she was determined to help him learn to walk again, and to help him admit that he could feel something, anything, even if it was nothing more than pressure on his legs.

And if you get your wish, what then? What if he goes back to rodeo? What will you do then?

She wouldn't think about that right now. It was easier to distract herself by rolling off him to snuggle next to his chest. His arms were still beneath her, his body turned so that he was half bent over her.

"How about you?" he asked softly. "Are you ready for what I have planned for *you* tonight?"

"I am," she said.

And she was.

Chapter Fifteen

She snuck away in the wee hours of the morning. She knew she shouldn't, knew that Trent might be offended when he woke up alone, but she did it anyway, dressing quickly, slipping from his cabin and into her truck before he woke up.

Coward.

Good Lord, it was crazy how he'd made her feel.

Gingerly, she started the truck. The sun had just come up over the horizon, creating a pale glow in the sky. Behind her, the tires kicked up a tiny plume of dust, but Trent didn't burst out of his cabin, blanket thrown over his midsection, wheelchair skidding to a halt in the middle of the road.

Whew. Made it.

And later? What then?

She would cross that bridge when she came to it, she told herself firmly. Maybe all he'd wanted was a one-night stand, like she had, because there was no way they could ever repeat what happened last night. She was his therapist, for goodness' sake. She should have never, ever crossed the line between therapist and patient.

Except...

It hadn't felt wrong when they'd been in bed together. It had felt amazingly right. They'd made love two more times—a record for her, although maybe not for him. He'd probably had lots of partners back when he'd been a rodeo star. He might have a score of partners again once he went back to the circuit—

Stop!

She would not think about that. She needed to focus on getting back to her house before Cabe realized where she'd been all night, not that he'd have a problem with her and Trent, she just didn't want him knowing they'd hooked up, and she definitely didn't want Rana to know. If the girl spotted her sneaking back into her home, not only would Alana be mortified, but she worried Rana might read something into it that wasn't there, like Alana maybe falling in love and leaving her....

Never.

She didn't go back to bed. There was no way she could sleep. Instead she took a long, leisurely shower, getting to the barn well ahead of Cabe. She threw herself into mucking stalls, so that when Cabe came up behind her and asked, "You going to tell me where you scurried off to yesterday?" she almost dropped the rake.

"Good heavens, you scared the heck out of me." She turned to face him, the handle clutched to her chest. "Don't sneak up on me like that."

Her best friend stared at her as if she were a cat that'd knocked over a bowl of water. "Boy, staying out makes you jumpy."

Did he know? Had he guessed? Alana studied his face, searching for clues, but all she spotted was a teasing glint in his eyes.

"It was a long drive back." She realized her mouth had gone dry and had to swallow a few times in order for her vocal cords to start working. "I took him to the Reno Rodeo."

Quickly, she explained what had happened, and how she hoped they'd had a breakthrough. She made no mention of spending the night with him. Nor did she attempt to explain why she driven the truck up to the house so early in the morning, and he didn't ask.

"Glad it worked out." He smiled. "Got a minute? I thought we could go over next week's schedule."

She must have shrunk three inches, her relief was so great. He wasn't going to push the issue, thank goodness.

"Sure."

She followed him to his office above the barn by the stairwell in a back corner. Their footfalls echoed off the narrow landing above, a single frosted-glass door opening into his work space. It wasn't big—they used most of the barn's attic area for storing hay—but it was big enough. As large as her apartment. Arched windows spaced at regular intervals allowed light to pour onto the hardwood floor. Skylights had been built into the ceiling space, giving the room a soft, airy feel. This was where Cabe conducted the business of running a dude ranch. Speaking of which...

"Did you purposely not book any guests for last week and this week?"

The question had been bothering her for days now. It was mid-June, a time that was usually quiet until school let out, but not *this* quiet.

Cabe nodded. "From everything I heard, I thought Trent might need some privacy, but someone called this morning. A family with a disabled child. I'm thinking I'll go ahead and book them in since you're doing so well with him."

She nodded, though she had to work to keep her features from giving the game away. Cabe would fall over in shock if he knew what that privacy had led to last night.

Instead, she asked, "When do they want to come?"

"Maybe tomorrow, maybe next week." He turned to his computer, pressed some keys. "I need to call them back. As for Trent's sessions, are you going to continue with the same type of therapy? More riding? Or are you planning more unscheduled trips to rodeos?"

"I think we'll keep it to the riding. He seemed to do great the other day."

When he met her gaze, the teasing glint was back in his eyes. "I know. I saw the two of you looking pretty cozy there at the end of the soccer lesson the other day."

A flash fire broke out across her cheekbones. "That was nothing. I was just, ah, grateful that he'd agreed to help Rana. That's all."

"Uh-huh," Cabe teased.

"No. Really."

He laughed. "Honestly, Alana, I wouldn't care if the two of you had driven off to Reno to get married—"

"Cabe!"

"Well, maybe I would mind." He winked. "I'd at least expect an invitation."

"You're kidding, right?"

"Of course I am." He shook his head. "My point being that you've been living like a nun ever since my brother's passing. Maybe it's time to move on. You should know I'm okay with that."

He *did* know. He had to. Why else would they be having this conversation?

She waited for him to say something more, something about driving the truck up to the house so early in the morning, and when he didn't, she said, "I could say the same about you."

His amusement faded. The top of his desk became the object of his attention, but only for a second or two. "Point taken, but here's the major difference. I think you like Trent."

She leaned back in her chair. Frankly, she was surprised she didn't fall over backward in shock. "Excuse me? I just met the man."

Cabe didn't have to say a word. He didn't need to. She'd seen that look on his face before. It was the same expression he used on Rana when she'd told him she'd do her homework right after she rode Scooter, instead of before, which the girl knew would never fly. Still, that didn't stop Rana from trying.

"The man has more baggage than a New York heiress."

"So do you."

"I do not."

"They why haven't you been on a date in years?"

"Why haven't you?"

"Busy." He smiled.

"Me, too."

"Bull," he said, leaning forward. "That hay grower out of Klamath. That man has asked you out at least a half-dozen times. Shoot, the girls at the feed store told me he's crazy about you. You could go into town and have a quick lunch with him, or dinner, or something."

She pressed her lips together in a frown. "I'd rather be here working with guests than out dating some strange man."

"That's just it." He pointed in accusation. "The hay grower's no stranger, and neither is Trent."

"He is, too."

"How is he a stranger when you've been watching him on TV for years?"

He teased her, although not without some seriousness, but unbeknownst to him, his words had the opposite effect. What if he did get better? What if he did return to the sport of rodeo? That would be great.

She almost sighed.

That would be *wonderful*…but not for her, for so many reasons, least of which was her commitment to the ranch.

"I'm just saying you should think about it."

"And you should think about it, too."

"I will."

"Fine. I will, too."

"So when do you plan to put him up on a horse again?"

She took a deep breath, tried not to think about how awkward she would feel facing Trent after…after…well, just after.

"I'm not sure. Today, maybe. I was thinking a little aqua therapy might be good." Man, she wished she could smack the smirk off his face.

"The hot springs?"

Being only a stone's throw away from a volcanic park had its advantages. Hot springs were everywhere. If you drove out toward Elko, Nevada, in the early morning hours, plumes of steam could be seen everywhere.

"It should be an easy ride."

"A little wine, a little warm water—"

She tossed a Post-it notepad at his head. She hadn't even known she was going to do it until the thing flew in his direction.

"Hey." He thrust his hands in front of him as if she might throw something else, and she just might.

"Please stay on topic. I was about to say the past couple of days have undoubtedly taken their toll on his muscles, even if he can't feel it," she said, a part of her wondering if he was sore after last night. *She* was—

"You think he can make it?"

She snapped back to the present. "I don't think it'll be a problem, and I really think he needs it. I also think he suffers from conversion disorder. The other day, his calf, the one that supposedly had a phantom pain? It had a knot in it, a knot the size of an egg."

"Really?"

"He feels things. There's just a disconnect in there somewhere. I think he realizes that now, mentally, at least. I need to build on that today."

Cabe was nodding. "Good. I think you're on the right track."

He changed the subject to the following week and the guests coming in, but it was all Alana could do to focus.

What if she was wrong? What if last night had been nothing more than a fluke?

You're being silly.

Maybe, but she couldn't shake the feeling that she still had a long way to go to heal Trent. As far as their relationship went...

She gulped.

With any luck, he would understand she regretted their impulsive actions. She would explain that it couldn't happen again. He was at New Horizons Ranch so she could help him, not sleep with him.

Too bad she had a feeling he wasn't going to take no for an answer.

SHE'D DITCHED HIM.

Trent didn't know why it bothered him, but it did. Probably because in the past he'd had to practically push women out the door. Not that he indulged in one-night stands very often, but when he did, there was almost always that awkward moment, the one that happened when two people who'd shared a night realized they had nothing in common.

That wouldn't be the case with Alana.

And so he'd experienced something close to disappointment when he'd awoken to find her gone. Shoving that feeling aside, he hefted himself into his chair and studied his legs beneath the edge of his boxers. He hated the scars, he thought, tracing an angry red line that ran from his knee up his thigh, not that they seemed to bother Alana. But despite Alana's reassurances, he felt nothing, just the rough puckering of skin and a keen sense of loss.

Damn. Where had she gone?

He dressed and shaved as quickly as he could, found his cowboy hat hanging next to the door and crammed it on. He had a pretty good idea where he'd find her.

It was still early morning, the scent of pine and sage filling the air, the quiet call of the creek fading behind him. Shadows created by the tall pine trees reached out for him, swallowing him up only to release him back to the sun an instant later. It was beautiful here, he admitted, almost as pretty as Colorado, but nothing could beat his hometown's blue skies and craggy vistas. Nothing.

His wheels crackled over the dirt path, Trent's heart rate accelerating with each passing moment, although not because of the exercise. The more he thought about it, the more he wondered if she regretted what happened last night.

She was right where he thought she'd be, working in the barn. The sound of the rake she ran across the barn's hard-packed dirt aisle masked his wheels.

"I would never have figured you to be the love 'em and leave 'em type."

Her eyes instantly widened, and Trent spotted the telltale signs of discomfort: color blooming along her cheeks, lips trying to smile, eyes that met his own, but only for a second.

"Good morning," she said brightly.

No trespassing. Keep twenty feet away. Use caution. If her body had been a road sign, that's what it would have said.

He wheeled himself closer, peering at her from beneath the brim of his hat. He pitched his voice low. "I was disappointed to find myself alone this morning."

"Oh, ah, yeah. About that..."

He watched her swallow, a part of him thinking she put every buckle bunny he'd ever met to shame. She was one of those women who looked just as good with her hair pulled back—as it was now—or loose and down her back. This morning her eyes were as startling as the Colorado sky he loved so much, the combination of sexy woman, cowgirl attire and shy lover one that he'd never encountered before.

"I thought you could use the sleep."

She wore a white shirt, the color reflecting ambient light back onto her face. A photographer would love the way that light combined with the dust around her to create a backdrop that looked like something out of a magazine spread.

"Are you kidding? That's all I've been doing for months. Eating, sleeping, getting up, eating, sleeping and then doing it all over again." He gave her a smile.

She set the rake down. "Okay, so, about last night."

Funny how his breathing could simply stop.

"I'm not certain our, ah...interlude was such a wise idea."

He could tell that just by the way she was looking at him. "Interlude?"

"I'm not— I mean, I never..." She looked heavenward. As if the words she sought might be whispered in her ear by the Great Almighty. "I don't usually do that with, um, actually, I've *never* done anything like that with a guest."

"I'm glad to hear it." He rolled his chair forward, then back again, admitting to himself he had a bad case of nerves. "I would hate to think you made a habit of it."

She glanced upward again, and Trent suddenly realized she looked that way because Cabe's office was up there.

"I just think that maybe, um, you know, we shouldn't have done it. What if someone puts two and two together? Not very professional of me to, ah, to do *that*."

"It's not like you forced me."

She drew back. "I know. I just worry that you'll be gone in a couple of weeks."

"Says who?"

"You mean you might stay?"

To be honest, he hadn't given tomorrow, forty-eight hours from now, or even next week, a single thought.

"I don't know." He shrugged his shoulders. "Can't we just take it day by day?"

Clearly, she didn't know how to respond to that question. "Well, I—"

"It's not like I'm proposing marriage or something."

The words made him feel funny inside, as if he shouldn't be teasing her about such a thing, although hell if he knew why. Or maybe he did. Maybe it had something to do with the fact that it'd been months, nearly a year, since he'd felt anything other than despair clogging his throat, and now here he was, with Alana, a woman who'd reminded him last night that there was more to life than a wheelchair.

"No, of course not."

He wheeled himself forward and back again. "Good. We're agreed." He placed his hands on his lap. "So what've you got planned for me today?"

Clearly, she wanted to continue the conversation. Just as clearly, she wasn't certain what to say, or how to convince him that she wanted to forget last night had ever happened. That was what she was really thinking—he could tell. He'd just have to convince her otherwise.

"I was thinking we could take a trip to the hot springs."

"Sounds good." Sounded really good, actually.

"How are your legs this morning?"

As a change of subject, it was as good as any, he supposed. He let her get away with it. "Same as always."

She frowned. "No improvement?"

"Not that I'm aware of."

"That will change."

She sounded so positive, so completely sure of herself, he was half tempted to believe her. Funny how she could be so certain about one thing, but not about another.

"Then let's get to it."

She nodded, obviously pleased by his easy agreement, and the fact that he wasn't rolling up to her, sweeping her into his lap and kissing her senseless, which was something he'd been wanting to do since he'd spotted her in the barn. Instead, he kept out of her way as she led their horses to the cross-ties, although, to be honest, he paid more attention to the sexy sway of her hips than what she was doing with the horses. When she finished, she led the same bay gelding that he'd ridden before out into the June sunshine. He followed behind, half tempted to roll up behind her and smack her in the butt, just to see what she would do. The only blight on his horizon was the stupid rocking chair saddle she'd strapped on the back of the bay horse.

"You know, I really hate that thing."

She led Baylor toward the parallel bars. She didn't look back as she said, "I know you do, but we can't take a chance, not until you build more muscle."

"I can think of one way to build more muscle."

She paused, met his gaze, the sun illuminating her eyes. They were huge. Her best feature with the wide, sweeping brows that framed them so perfectly.

"Ha, ha, ha," she said.

He turned toward the ramp, spotting the saddle as he reached the top of the platform. "How about we ditch the straps?"

"Nope." She had stopped, holding Baylor's reins so he could mount. "Don't want you to fall off."

That got him to move, although not toward the horse—toward the edge of the platform. He saw Alana's whole body tense when she spotted the wicked gleam in his eyes. He stopped a mere few inches away, Baylor turning his head as if hoping for a treat.

"What if *you* fall?" He leaned toward her. *"For me?"*

Chapter Sixteen

He didn't mean that. He was just teasing her. Of course she wouldn't fall for him. It'd just been a one-night stand. A momentary lapse in judgment.

A big lapse, she corrected herself.

"Ha, ha," she said again.

She didn't like him teasing her. It made her feel all weird inside.

Googly.

Like a swarm of gnats fluttered around her belly.

"You never know." He smiled down at her. "Stranger things could happen."

"Why don't we focus on you not falling off Baylor right now?" She stoked the big bay. Good Lord, she hoped he didn't see the way her cheeks flushed with color.

He liked her.

Stupid. So what? She'd spent most of the morning thinking about him—and why a relationship with him was out of the question. She went over that list now as she held Baylor so he could mount.

Lives in another state. Check.

Has major emotional baggage. Check. Check.

Might be latching on to her for all the wrong reasons. Check. Check. Check.

"Let's go," she heard him say.

What if this was some kind of Florence Nightingale thing?

What if it was a Florence Nightingale thing for *her?* What if she had confused her desire to help him with a different kind of desire? Dang it. Why had she jumped into bed with him?

She went to her own horse, still cross-tied inside the barn, and blinked against the sudden darkness. In seconds she was beside Trent, a part of her admitting he looked good sitting atop Baylor in jeans and cowboy boots and his beige cowboy hat.

"I feel like one of those elephant riders," he said. "You know, the ones that sit in those weird saddles? Or maybe it's camel riders."

"Just focus on using your legs."

He shot her a sexy grin. "I can think of one way to use my legs that's a whole hell of a lot better than riding a horse."

Ignore him.

"Yeah, right." Although she had no idea if she meant the words for herself, or for him.

Either way, it was hard. Riding alongside him, having him right next to her, for all intents and purposes like a normal man, it made her think of things. Scary things. What if she did help him? What if she helped him to overcome his mental disabilities. What if he went back to the rodeo circuit?

Could you care for someone else again? Even if it meant leaving Rana and the ranch?

She shooed the thoughts away. It was too soon to be thinking that way. They barely knew each other. Sure, last night had been wonderful and remarkable and unforgettable, but if that was all there ever was between them, she could be happy with that.

Couldn't she?

Because the truth was she really liked this man. Sure, he'd started out as an ass, but she'd also witnessed his softer side, not just last night, but with Rana and the rodeo fans, too.

"Let's trot," she said.

"Ah, do we have to?"

"Yes."

Trotting was one way to keep her mind off things.

She kicked her horse forward, and damned if Trent didn't handle himself well. He looked perfectly poised atop Baylor. Occasionally, she saw him clutch the horse's mane as they made their way around trees and up the gentle incline, but he really could use those legs far more than a man with his supposed degree of disability. He'd done so last night, too, but he seemed to have slipped back into his original frame of mind— paralyzed from the thighs down—because he was bouncing around like a sack of potatoes.

Damn.

She pulled her horse up, took a deep breath. If she were to help him, really truly help him, she needed to get to the bottom of things.

"Why are you afraid to walk again?"

"Excuse me?"

Behind him, already far in the distance, sat New Horizons Ranch, looking smaller than it really was, and like an oasis in a sea of light-and-dark-green patches of trees.

"You can use your legs, Trent. You did last night. Now you can't. Or you think you can't. So what's blocking you?"

She turned her horse to face him. Up ahead, the path they followed disappeared into trees with tall blades of grass on either side of the road dancing to the tune of a small breeze.

"Didn't we have this conversation before?"

"Not really." She stroked Radical's mane, the black strands falling through her fingers like corn silk. "Sort of."

"Nothing changed last night." He patted his own horse. "Sure, I stood up for a moment or two, but that doesn't mean anything."

"Doesn't it?" She took a deep, fortifying breath. "Didn't last night prove to you that you were capable of more than you thought?"

He studied the scenery below them, shrugging before he said, "I don't know. I'm half inclined to believe that was a fluke. Believe me. I checked my legs this morning and they still feel the same as before."

She sighed. "You really think that, don't you?"

He nodded.

"Well, if that's what you think, why don't we put it to a test?"

"What do you mean?"

She grabbed his horse's reins before he could protest, the two leads sliding through his fingers, although he managed to hold on to the tail end of them. Baylor knew the drill. The moment she clucked, he trotted, and when she kept on clucking, cantered.

"Hey!" He tried to pull back. "Not this again."

"We're going to do way more than trot this time."

"What?"

"Hold on."

Her conscience twanged, but only for a moment. He'd be all right, just as he had been at the trot. The saddle would hold him no matter what happened; she was the one who had to keep an eye out for stray rocks and holes.

"Just use your legs."

Believe, she silently urged.

"Alana—"

She glanced back at him, nearly smiling at the fear mixed with dismay on his face, but she urged Baylor and her horse into a lope just the same. As she suspected, the saddle did its job. Twenty feet, forty, the rhythmic thuds of their horses' hooves kicking up tiny dust plumes.

He must have realized he wasn't going to fall off because when she next glanced back she could tell he'd started to relax, the irritated flexing of his jaw fading away. And his legs. They weren't flopping around anymore. Not at all.

"Look at your legs," she said, pointing.

He glanced down, shook his head.

"You're using them."

He didn't look convinced, but he couldn't see them, at least not without leaning to the side, something she knew he wasn't about to do.

"Let's go faster," she said.

"No."

She ignored him. He tried to gather up the reins, but she had too firm a grip on Baylor to be effective.

"Yee-haa!" She cued her horse into a run.

"Alana!"

He held on. By God the man rode just as well at a run as he did the slow canter. Most important, he was using his legs. They clutched his horse's sides like a trick rider. The road raced beneath them, and she closed her eyes for a second at the sheer joy helping him made her feel. This was why she did what she did, why she kept to herself at the ranch, why she would never leave. When she opened her eyes again it was to glance back and make sure he still did okay.

She smiled.

The man wore a fierce look of concentration on his face; it turned his eyes dark, caused his jaw to thrust forward. She'd seen that look before, but only ever on TV, and only just before he'd been about to nod his head seconds before he burst from a chute.

"You're doing gr—"

"Watch out!"

She jerked forward, gasped.

Tree branch.

She ducked. Too late.

Bark dug into her shoulder. The impact knocked her sideways. She tried to cling to Radical's back. No use. She hit the ground. Hard.

"Alana!"

She tried to call out, couldn't, and felt herself collapse.

"Damn, damn, damn." The reins. Trent used everything he had to lean forward and reach for them. "Whoa," he called, drawing back on the slack.

Baylor slowed.

"Whoa," he ordered again, tugging on the reins this time. The gelding instantly obeyed. One more tug and the big gelding stopped.

"Come on," he told the horse, jerking the reins toward Alana.

She hadn't moved.

He kicked Baylor forward, giving it all that he had. Damn it, he couldn't seem get there fast enough.

"Alana," he called again.

With a thud of hooves on dirt, he finally made it back to her side. Trent jerked Baylor to a stop only inches away from where she lay. Her eyes were still closed, and a gash oozed blood on her forehead.

Bleeding.

His hands made quick work of the buckle around his waist, but once finished, fear overtook him. He couldn't do it. There was no way he could get off the horse on his own. No way at all.

Sickened, he ran through his options. Race back to the ranch. Get help there. But he'd have to leave her behind. What if she had internal bleeding? What if she had brain damage?

Did she have a cell phone?

Surely she did. Why hadn't he grabbed his?

Minutes counted.

It would take minutes to race back to the ranch. Minutes more if Cabe wasn't at the barn. Even more minutes if someone was in the house and couldn't hear him shouting.

"Shit."

Before he could think better of it, he undid the buckles around his legs, then clutched Baylor's mane and flung himself off.

He nearly fell to the ground.

"Alana," he called again.

Still no movement.

You can do this.

Just like last night, he forced himself to balance, forced himself to wedge his legs beneath him. Baylor, trouper that he was, didn't move. He used the horse's neck as a balancing bar, forced his hips to move, his legs to swing. One step. Two. Three. She was right beneath him.

He let go.

He didn't fall.

What the—

He stood. On his own.

But only for a moment because then he collapsed next to her. "Alana."

Still no movement.

He began to search her pockets. "Where the hell did you put it?" he muttered, his hands running down her pockets. "You have to have one somewhere."

"Have what?"

He rocked back on his knees. Or he tried to. In their weakened state, his thighs couldn't quite manage the movement.

"Shit," he cried as he fell backward.

"Trent?" She slowly sat up, her pretty blue eyes meeting his gaze.

He held out his hands toward her. "Don't move."

She touched her shoulder, winced. "I hit it." And then of all the crazy things, she started to laugh. "I hit the damn tree."

"You have a gash on your head."

She brushed the wound with her fingers. "Just a scratch."

"It's bleeding. We should call 911. Where's your cell phone?"

"A stupid tree." She winced again. "I can't believe I did that."

"Are you hurt anywhere else?"

"I'm fine." Her gaze hooked his like a harpoon. "You got off Baylor all on your own." She went from laughing to serious in the space of an instant. "Trent, do you know what this means?"

He smirked. "I'm better at getting off a horse than you are?"

She went back to smiling again. "You did it."

"Only because I had to. Come on. Let's get you back on your horse. We need to get you to a doctor."

"I don't need to see a doctor. I'm fine." She pushed herself up. "Look at you."

Yeah, look at him. Weak. Sitting on his rear, propping his

upper body up with his arms, while she stared at him with a bloody gash on her forehead.

"Alana, I'm not joking. Give me your cell phone so I can call 911."

"No."

"You were unconscious."

"No, I wasn't." She shook her head in a self-deprecating fashion. "I just had the wind knocked out of me. Took me a minute to catch my breath."

"Your brain could be swelling."

She twisted around so that she sat next to him. "Would you stop it, Trent? I'm fine. There's not even a bump." She touched her forehead again. "I got whipped by the branch."

"What's your name?"

She rolled her eyes. "Madonna."

He shot her a look that clearly said, *ha, ha, ha.* "What's to-day's date?"

She tipped her head sideways and smiled. "The day you got off a horse all on your own."

"Alana—"

"Shh." She moved toward him, placed a hand on his lips. "I'm all right."

But she seemed to regret the gesture the moment she touched him, because she snatched her hand away. He grabbed it back.

"You scared the crap out of me." The gash really wasn't a gash, he admitted. It was, as she'd said, just a scratch. He could see that now. "I thought you'd blacked out when you didn't answer me."

"I couldn't breathe. You know how it is. Lungs compressing and forcing the air out. Takes a minute for them to fill back up."

He did, indeed, know the feeling well. He studied her face, seeing the truth in her eyes. She turned, scouted around for her horse. The animal hadn't gone far. "At least we don't have to go hunting for Radical."

"You certain you're okay?"

"Fine." He watched as she forced a grin onto her face. "Let's see if you've gotten any feeling back in your legs, too." She reached for them.

"No."

She drew back. "But you believe me now, don't you, Trent? You're not as bad as you think. You just need to believe. Up here." She tapped her head.

He didn't know what to believe.

You jumped off a horse.

All right, so he hadn't exactly flung himself off like the Lone Ranger, but damned if he hadn't done it. That was twice now he'd used his legs when he would have sworn it was impossible.

"Can you help me up?"

Her eyes brightened. "Going to try standing again?"

He held out a hand. She stood, saying, "Wait." Then she ran to grab Baylor so he could use the horse to steady himself. "Here."

She held out a hand. He took it, pulling himself to his feet, and though he'd done so twice, a part of him still marveled.

He did it.

He wobbled a bit, had to clutch Baylor's saddle for assistance and then lean on the side of his horse for support, but he did it.

"I don't get it." He was weak, sure, but apparently he could stand on his own. What did that mean?

Her grip tightened around his hand. "Can I have a look at them?"

Though he didn't expect any different results than before, he said, "Go ahead." He kept standing. He was afraid to move, afraid he'd lose his balance and fall.

"Here." She let go of his hand, squatting down and touching just above his left knee, the spot that had always been numb since the accident. "Can you feel that?"

Could he? He forced himself to concentrate. "Maybe."

"This?" She squeezed his knee.

He was starting to feel something, all right, but it had nothing to do with his knee. Actually, it had everything to do with the way she touched him.

"How about the other leg?" She repeated the process.

And maybe he did feel something. Maybe…

Whatever it was, it faded beneath the sight of her kneeling down at his feet, and it amazed him, really, that all it took was watching her do something mundane, like stroking his knee, to get him going.

"Anything?" She glanced up at him, her ponytail cascading over one shoulder, the shape of her face so perfect he found himself wanting to study it. If she wore makeup, he couldn't tell.

"Honey, what I'm feeling has nothing to do with my legs."

Her mouth formed an O of surprise before she stood again, but she clutched a hand to her head as if it suddenly hurt.

"Are *you* okay?" he asked.

"I'm fine. No little headache will get me down, not when I think we're finally seeing some progress."

Were they?

"Look." His gaze moved away from hers. It was stunning up in the mountains, he admitted, surveying the ranch less than five miles away, the slanted slope of the barn, the patchwork of pastures, the Feather River snaking its way through the valley and glistening like a ribbon of liquid silver. Cabe and Rana appeared to be riding below. He spotted Cabe's black cowboy hat and Rana's petite frame. "No matter what happens—" he glanced down at his legs "—if this is as good as it gets, I can't thank you enough for everything."

"This isn't as good as it's going to get." Her eyes grew intense, as if she tried to telepathically transfer her determination into his mind. "You wouldn't be able to stand like this if you didn't have at least *some* muscle control."

"I do have muscles that work. You know that. Some of my thigh muscles. I must be learning to use them better."

"No. It's more than that."

He dropped his hand, stroking the side of her face as he smiled. "I think if you could will me to walk again, you would."

She looked away with a smile. "I would."

"No sacrifice too great for my recovery, huh?"

She laughed softly, and he admitted that she gave him hope. "Have you helped many others?" he asked. "Like me?"

She worried her bottom lip before answering, and for some reason, the gesture made him want to pull her to him and kiss her.

"Not as many as I would have liked." She, too, studied the scenery below. "Rana was my biggest success. Sure, I do a lot of therapy here, but never a case like yours, someone whose issues might be more mental than physical."

"I still don't think that's necessarily true."

"I do, Trent. I really do." She peered up at him intently. "I believe that you can do whatever you set your mind to do—if you just believe in yourself."

He marveled; that was the only way to describe how she made him feel. "You are so amazing."

She huffed out a laugh in a self-deprecating fashion. "No, I assure you, I'm not."

"Yes, you are." But he spotted how she blushed on the heels of his compliment. "Have you ever thought about leaving the ranch? You know, expanding your horizons?"

"No." She said the word so quickly and so firmly that he knew he'd hit a nerve. "I'll never leave here. Never abandon Rana. Not ever."

Abandon Rana? So she'd clearly taken over as the mother figure in the girl's life. Not surprising, he thought, given her big heart. He could see her stepping in and taking care of a lot of things.

"What if it was only part of the year? You know, during winter, when the ranch surely shuts down."

"Actually, it doesn't. Cabe rents cabins to hunters, but that's beside the point. Christmas is…special around here. I could never leave."

The finality in those words gave him pause. After last night he'd thought... Well, they could *still* have a future, he reassured himself, if they wanted. Sure, it might be a little too early in the game to be thinking such thoughts. Then again, maybe not. Alana was unlike any woman he'd ever met before. Quite frankly, she blew him away with her tenacious desire to help others and her willingness to do whatever it took, even when it came time to help persnickety assholes like himself.

"We should leave," she said, stepping away from him. "I think I should maybe get a Band-Aid on my head."

"It wasn't just a fling for me, you know."

She straightened suddenly.

"I'm not that kind of guy." He shook his head. "I've never been that kind of guy."

She stared at him. "Never?"

He knew he spoke the truth, and so he had no trouble meeting her gaze. "Never."

She didn't look away, no doubt studying him for signs that he lied. But then her face crumpled. He reached for her. She stepped away.

"Damn you, Trent Anderson, I liked you better when you weren't nice to me."

"That wasn't the real me."

She peered up at him again. "I know," she said softly. "I think I knew that from the moment you arrived. I've read the stories. Heard about the charities you support, still support. You're not the evil ogre you make yourself out to be."

He had feelings for her, he admitted. Remarkable feelings, given he'd only known her such a short time. Last night had changed everything for him.

"Don't let my disabilities scare you away."

She laughed, actually laughed. "That would never make me afraid."

"Then what is it? Why do I sense this...resistance?"

She shook her head. "You don't understand, Trent. This

ranch. What I do here—it's my whole life. There's no room for anything else."

"Bull."

She glanced up at him sharply. "It's not bull. It's the truth."

"Have you ever even tried?"

"I haven't had the time."

"Then do it. With me."

He couldn't believe he said the words. It was too soon. He would scare her off.

"Would you be willing to move?" she asked quietly.

Uproot from Colorado? "I don't know. Maybe."

But she wasn't paying any attention to him, not anymore; her gaze had moved past him, her brow furrowed. "Who's that?"

He didn't want to look away, didn't want the moment to end, wanted to get to the bottom of whatever this was between them, but he followed her gaze anyway, spotting the horse and rider almost instantly. *Two* horses and two riders, the ones he'd spotted earlier, only it wasn't Cabe and Rana.

Son of a—

"Is that Saedra?" Alana asked.

No, not just Saedra. His former roping partner, Mac McKenzie, too.

"Damn."

Chapter Seventeen

"Well, well, well," Saedra said as she pulled a fancy-looking bay gelding to a stop, the horse's coat shining like a copper penny in the afternoon sunlight. "Look who's standing on his own two feet again."

Thank God for the interruption. Thank God because the look in Trent's eyes had…

What?

Scared the hell out of her. She couldn't believe she'd actually asked him if he would move. What was wrong with her? Even if he was willing to do that, it was a little early to be having those kinds of thoughts.

"And this time without the benefit of an audience," Mac McKenzie said, squishing his hat down on his head as he pulled a sorrel gelding to stop. "Good for you, bud."

Alana glanced at Trent. He didn't look pleased to see his two friends. "What are you guys doing here?"

"Thought I'd stick around a couple extra days," Saedra said. "Wasn't hard to spot the two of you climbing up the hill."

Her eyes darted between the two of them, curiosity clearly shining from her eyes. "Your friend Cabe pointed you out." The pretty blonde frowned. "Although I think he'd have preferred if we waited around, but I insisted we ride out. Asked Mr. Jensen why bother waiting when we had two perfectly good horses we could unload and ride? So we did."

"Actually, we were just headed back that way." Alana

touched her head. "I had an argument with a tree." She forced a smile to her lips though her heart still pounded from her encounter with Trent. "Tree won."

"Are you okay?" Saedra asked.

"Fine."

"Well, good thing we came along when we did," Mac said.

"What made you want to stick around?" Trent asked Saedra.

"I'm hauling Saedra's new horse back to Colorado for her," Mac interjected.

"My new NFR horse," Saedra said, patting the bay's black mane. "Can you believe it? I've had my eye on Jake for years, but I never thought she'd sell him. Thank God I flew to Reno for the rodeo."

And there she had it. All the reason in the world why a relationship with Trent would never work. The NFR. Rodeo. A life on the road.

Never again.

Clearly, though, the news brought joy to Trent, because he smiled, though it was a hard-fought battle for him, too. She could tell. Clearly he would have liked to have continued their conversation.

So he could speak to you about the future.

"So, you heading back?" Mac asked.

"We are," Alana answered for the two of them.

"You need some help getting back on your horse?" Mac eyed Baylor skeptically. "Don't rightly know how you got down."

"Determination," Trent grumbled under his breath.

Mac must have heard. "Well, it'll take that to get you back up, I suspect."

In actuality it took a tree stump, Mac lifting, Saedra holding everyone's horses, and Alana guiding Baylor to get Trent aboard what Mac called the "damnedest-looking saddle he'd ever seen," although she noticed Trent left the buckles undone.

"Are you sure you want to do that?" she asked him.

He glanced down at her, determination in his gaze. "Gotta try it sometime."

"How about you?" Saedra asked. "You okay to ride with that head of yours?"

"Peachy."

And she was. To be honest, she was more rattled by the undercurrents between her and Trent than anything else. What had he been about to agree to? What if he'd said he'd move? Would that be so bad?

Dear Lord, she wasn't certain she was ready for that. Even after all this time, the thought of jumping into a relationship again scared the crap out of her.

Cabe had been right. She *was* a coward.

"Off we go," Saedra said, shooting everyone a grin.

From somewhere, Alana found the energy to muster up an answering smile, while Mac quizzed Trent on his saddle as they rode along.

A saddle that he might no longer need.

"Gonna toss some loops with me later on?" she heard Mac ask. "Looks like y'all have a nice roping arena."

Alana nodded, but she was distracted by her thoughts, so much so that the ride back down to the ranch passed in a blur.

"...do you?"

"I'm sorry? What?"

Saedra, who had clearly just asked her a question, grinned. "I asked if you thought the owner of the ranch would mind us spending a night or two."

"Cabe?" Alana glanced up, realizing they were very nearly to the main pasture now, the morning having passed into early afternoon, at least judging by the angle of the shadows thrown down by the fence posts.

"I'm sure he'll be fine with that," she said when Saedra nodded. "We might even have a cabin for you. Worst case, I'm sure you can stay at the main house."

When she glanced over at the blonde, it was to note the lifted brows. "The actual house?"

"Yeah, sure. Why not?"

Saedra shook her head, her pretty hair catching the sunlight. Really, the woman was gorgeous beyond belief.

"I just don't think—well, your boss seemed sort of put out when we showed up." Saedra squinted as she stared straight ahead, as if looking for evidence of Cabe in the buildings. "His daughter was nice enough. She was thrilled to meet Mac."

I bet. Once a rodeo fan, always a rodeo fan.

But Cabe? Out of sorts? The man was the epitome of hospitality.

"You must have caught him at a bad moment. Cabe's the nicest man I know."

"Is he your boyfriend?"

The thought was so foreign to her, she actually laughed, something that caught Trent's eyes because she saw him cast his gaze in their direction.

"Absolutely not."

Trent had paired up with Mac, the two of them discussing Mac's recent wins, from the sound of it.

"Yeah. I kind of guessed that was the case, especially judging by the way Trent was staring into your eyes earlier. He's not the type to poach on another man's property."

"Excuse me?"

"Don't bother to deny it." The woman was all smiles again. "I've known Trent my whole life. He's smitten."

She didn't know what to say, although her body certainly seemed to know how to react. She couldn't stop the blush that spread from her cheeks and down her neck, all the way to her belly, where it coiled before sending electric spasms of pleasure through her body.

Apparently, you're smitten, too.

No, she wasn't. She was just really, really attracted to him. Last night had proved that.

"It's not like that."

Oh, no? asked her subconscious. *One night of pleasure spent in the man's arms, and all you can think about is doing it again—to hell with the future.*

"Well, if it's not like that yet, it's sure headed in that direction. Trent really, really likes you. I can tell."

"He likes me because I'm helping him to walk again. That's all."

"Not true. He never looked at any of his other therapists the way he looks at you, and don't get me wrong. I couldn't be more thrilled. Honestly, I wasn't certain that coming here would be good for him, but I'm glad Gretchen insisted."

"Gretchen?"

"His mother."

Ah, yes. Their biggest advocate.

"Oh, damn," she heard Saedra say as they reached the gate near the backside of the barn. "*He's* still there."

"He" being Cabe. Alana had spotted him, too, oiling the saddles used by guests. And as she gazed between Saedra and Cabe, she couldn't help but forget about her own troubles. Sure enough, the moment her boss noticed Saedra's arrival, he straightened, shoulders thrown back, blue eyes narrowed.

"See," she heard Saedra say under her breath, "he doesn't like me."

"Impossible."

Yet Cabe, a man who prided himself on always greeting guests with a smile, didn't so much as lift one side of his mouth. Frankly, the horses inside the barn gave them more of a welcome, several of them nickering to the group of horses.

"Why are you back so early?" was all he said.

Okay, he nodded in Trent and Mac's direction, although not in Saedra's. *Strange.*

"I fell off," she replied.

His whole face underwent a transformation. "You what?"

"It was silly," she said, riding up to the back entrance of the barn. Mac, Trent and Saedra stopped behind her, their horses looking around curiously. "I was glancing back at Trent and I didn't see a tree."

Cabe dropped the rag he'd been using and came toward her,

sunlight bleaching his maroon-colored shirt to a lighter shade of red, black hat firmly in place. "You okay?"

"Fine," she said, dismounting and then glancing back at the group behind her. "Just a little scratch on my head."

"Let me see." Cabe gently clasped her chin, turning it this way and that.

"She's fine," Trent said. "I took a look at it earlier."

Cabe nodded, although whether in agreement or because he was satisfied that she wasn't about to fall over dead, she didn't know.

"Come on up to the office. I'll put some medicine on it."

"I think our guests still want to ride."

"They can do that on their own."

"I want to ride!"

From behind Cabe, Rana came flying out of the tack room, the rag she'd been using to clean saddles forgotten in her hand, twin brown ponytails streaming out behind her. "Maybe Trent can give me another lesson."

"Yeah, sure," she heard Trent say. "Mac can help you, too."

"Awesome!"

Saedra nudged her horse forward. "Are there some barrels I could use for practice?"

Cabe didn't even look in her direction.

"Yeah, sure," Alana answered for him. "They're in the shed at the back of the arena." She glanced between the two of them. "Rana can show you."

"Just give me a minute to saddle up," Rana said. The girl startled a small bird that had flown into the barn aisle in search of wheat kernels, she whipped around so fast.

The minute they were alone, she turned to Cabe. "What's gotten into you?"

"What do you mean?"

"What's your problem with Saedra?"

"Who?"

"Trent's friend. You seem mad at her."

"I'm not mad."

"No?"

The group of riders had disappeared around the side of the barn. She saw Cabe glance in their direction, a frown coming to his face.

"Cabe, you're not being straight with me. What's up?"

He shook his head. "Okay. Fine. She just rubbed me the wrong way."

"What'd she do?"

He shrugged. "Told me she was going to ride out after you even though I told her not to. Trent's roping partner didn't seem to have a problem staying behind, but that Saedra woman completely ignored me."

If she'd been wearing a cowboy hat, her eyebrows would have touched the brim, that was how much his words stunned her. Cabe was usually the embodiment of congeniality. Water ran off the man's back…usually.

"I just think she was anxious to see Trent."

Blue eyes shot to her own. "Is she his girlfriend?"

"No," Alana said.

Bizarrely enough, that seemed to calm him down a bit, although she doubted he noticed how his shoulders relaxed and his expression softened.

"She acted like she owned the place," pouted the thirty-five-year-old man.

"I have a feeling she's just that way."

Chapter Eighteen

A half hour later Alana had the same thought. Saedra Robbins was definitely a woman with her own opinions. Alana watched as she interacted with Rana. She wasn't bossy, per se. She was actually really helpful. She gave Rana some more exercises to use to control Scooter. Cabe had watched for two seconds before returning to office work.

What a grump.

His daughter, however, appeared to love the woman, but Alana couldn't keep her eyes off Trent as he walked his horse alongside Rana's. Scooter was so much better than that first day. He almost seemed like a different horse. Trent was full of reassuring smiles. He offered such sound advice that Alana thought again he'd make a great coach.

She could have it bad for the man.

There was no sense in denying it. If he would agree to move she might, just might, give a relationship with him a go. Might.

No doubt about it now that she'd had a few hours to puzzle it out. Jumping into a relationship with Trent scared the crud out of her. What if, God willing, she managed to help him walk again? What if he returned to the world of rodeo? What would she do then? Always on the road. Always traveling around.

Like Braden.

The pit in her stomach turned into a burning hole. Could she do it again? Could she be with a man who lived and breathed rodeo? Every once in a while, he'd glance in her direction…

like now. And her heart would stop, and she would think, why not? But then she would remember that life and how chaotic it had been, how all-consuming it'd been to have a boyfriend who competed for a living, how'd there been no time to herself...

"I think I'm ready to run a real pattern," Saedra announced.

"Cool!" Rana said.

It took a moment to set up the barrels the way Saedra wanted. She'd been practicing in a straight line, explaining to Rana that she rarely ran the barrel pattern the way it was set up at a rodeo.

"Here we go," Rana called as she scurried out of the arena and joined the crowd on the rail. Saedra guided her horse to the header box, the animal suddenly dancing beneath her. He knew what he was about to do. Sure enough, the minute Saedra turned to the barrels, her horse shot toward them like a guided missile.

"Wow," Rana cried.

The animal's ears pricked forward. The first barrel loomed. Saedra's blond hair streamed out behind her, like some kind of golden flag.

"Now, that's the way to break from the chute," Trent said.

She circled the first barrel. Perfectly. She crossed to the short side. They rounded the second one, turning toward the last barrel opposite where they stood. In the blink of an eye she was headed home, her horse's body seeming to lengthen and lower to the ground he ran so hard.

"Way to go, Saedra," Mac yelled as she pulled her horse up. "NFR, here she comes."

Saedra's grin had to be wide enough to see from space, her horse fighting the pressure of the reins, tossing its head, tail flicking back and forth. Clearly, he loved his job.

"That was so amazing to watch," Rana said.

"I can't believe I own this horse," she heard Saedra say, and if Alana didn't miss her guess, there were tears in her eyes. "I'm so grateful my business sold and I could afford him. And I'm so glad I came out here to see you, Trent, otherwise I would have never known about him being up for sale."

"See," Mac said, "it was meant to be."

"I'd make the girls on the high school rodeo circuit green with envy if I rode that horse," Rana said, seeming to sound almost disappointed that she'd never have that opportunity.

"Hey, maybe we should practice some roping, too," Mac offered. "I saw some steers in the front pasture. Mind if we push them in and throw a few loops?"

Alana's heart dropped to her toes.

Trent caught her gaze. He must have realized she didn't like that idea because he said, "I don't know if I'm up to that yet, and especially not in this saddle."

"Switch saddles," Mac said.

"You can borrow mine," Rana added.

"I don't even know if this horse knows how to rope." Trent glanced down at Baylor skeptically.

"He does," Rana said before Alana could interject. "All our horses are used for ranch work, too. He can head and heel, and drag a calf to the fire."

That was all Mac needed to hear. The big cowboy all but squirmed in the saddle. "Let's give it a try."

"Mac, I don't know if that's such a good idea." It was Saedra who came to Trent's rescue this time. "Yesterday was the first day Trent stood on his own two feet."

"He'll be fine." Apparently Mac didn't want to take no for an answer. "It's not like we're at a competition. We can take it slow."

"I don't know…" Saedra worried.

"Maybe in a few more days," Alana added.

The big man proved to be stubborn and Trent appeared torn between wanting to give it a try, and doing as Alana suggested.

"You want to use my saddle?" Rana asked.

Alana shook her head. "Rana, I think we should ask your dad, too."

"He won't mind, especially if you say it's okay." Rana turned to Alana.

All eyes shifted in her direction. Her cheeks filled with color, although goodness knew why. She only had Trent's best interest at heart. Right?

"Okay, fine." But her pulse raced. What if she was wrong? What if he really wasn't okay? What if this was too much for him? What if he fell…?

"He'll be fine," said the ever-confident Mac, the man obviously reading the expression on her face. But it was easy for him to say, she thought. Mac had to be over six feet tall, with matching shoulders and a neck the size of a prize bull. "I'll go with Rana to get the steers." Saedra fussed with her new horse's mane. "He needs a cooldown anyway."

Mac offered to loan Trent one of his saddles. Trent agreed, but the moment they were alone, he asked, "Do you think I'm ready for this?"

"Honestly, Trent, I don't know, but I guess we'll find out."

He nodded, turned his horse toward the gate. And that was that. In a few minutes they'd know, really, really know, if he was over his psychological block.

He used the ramp to get on and off, although he did that with greater and greater ease, she noticed, and he didn't use his chair to sit down, just held on to the railing. Progress. It should have filled her with elation, and it did. She couldn't be happier for him. But for some reason her heart had sunk to her belly, nausea causing her to take deep breaths—or was that nerves?

If he was all better, would he leave? Especially if she insisted he stay? He'd asked her if she could move away for part of the year, but she shook her head. She couldn't do that. This was her life. Cabe and Rana were her family. She'd worked hard for her independence since Braden's death—she wasn't about to give that up again.

"Ready?" she asked once he climbed into Mac's saddle. The setting sun behind him nearly blinded her, and Alana wondered where the day had gone. Shadows covered the ground beneath the pine trees, a cool breeze blew the blades of grass in the pasture left and then right. She wished she wore her own cowboy hat.

"I think I'm ready to go."

They locked eyes. She didn't know what to say, didn't know how to feel. This could be a turning point for him, she admitted, one that might lead him down a different path, a course that would take him away from her. Forever.

"Be careful."

But was she talking more to herself than Trent?

Be careful.

TRENT TOLD HIMSELF he should heed Alana's words. Mac's crazy idea to try his hand at roping could easily backfire. So far all he'd done was ride at a walk without his straps. Now he was in a different saddle, on a ranch horse, about to attempt something he hadn't done in nearly a year.

But it felt right.

As he walked toward the arena he admitted that he was more comfortable in Mac's roping saddle. The fact that he even felt anything at all had his heart pounding.

What if she were right? What if it'd been all in his head?

He would never ride bulls again, that was for sure. The doctors had warned him against reinjuring his back. Sure, there were rough-stock riders who'd broken their backs and recovered to ride again, but Trent knew those days were long behind him. That meant roping. One event. His best event, as luck would have it, but there would be no more all-around titles in his future.

Could he live with that?

The surge of excitement he felt was all the answer he needed, that and Mac's smile of encouragement. Alana could barely look him in the eye. Nerves, he supposed.

"I'm going to try trotting around first," he told his friend. "See how that goes."

Mac was busy twirling a rope, the nylon strands making a

whoosh, whoosh, whoosh as it spun through the air. The sight and sound caused Trent's palms to actually itch in anticipation. He wanted to twirl a rope, too.

"Good thinking," Mac said.

"Don't forget to use the horn if you need to," he heard Alana call out.

Squeeze, he told himself, sending the command down to his legs.

Baylor trotted.

Hot damn. It *had* worked.

"Don't go too fast," Alana cautioned.

She needn't have worried. It was like coming home again, his body instantly finding the horse's center of gravity, his legs lightly clutching the animal's side, or so it would appear because he wasn't flopping around, and he wasn't tilting to one side, either. He sat perfectly balanced. Held in place by his thighs. Maybe he didn't even need his calves.

"Whoa," he told the horse, leaning back.

Baylor instantly stopped.

"You sure don't ride like you're disabled."

It was Mac who'd spoken and Trent agreed. He didn't. Yes, he might be a little out of breath after trotting around for a minute, but that was to be expected.

"You ready for this?" Mac held up a rope.

"Yup." He took the nylon coils in his hand, testing the feel of them, uncoiling a loop, then recoiling it, then opening up a bigger loop before swinging it alongside Baylor to see how the animal would react. As Rana promised, the bay horse didn't bat an eye. He increased the size of his loop, brought it up and over his head.

And he wanted to cry.

It felt so good. So normal to be back on a horse again and twirling a rope. So perfect.

"I'm going to try loping."

It would be a true test, holding a rope in one hand, the reins in the other, all the while trying to stay on.

"Be careful," he heard Alana say.

He picked up his reins, thought the word *lope,* his legs doing…something, a something that Baylor must have felt because the well-trained horse instantly cantered off. He almost clutched the horn, resisted, told himself to relax, maybe to even close his eyes.

Feel the horse.

And he did.

He nudged Baylor's sides. Or rather, the fenders of the western saddle. The horse sped up a bit.

"Whoa."

Baylor instantly stopped.

"What's wrong?" Alana cried.

"I think my calves are working."

"What?"

He pulled Baylor around so that he faced Alana. "Baylor just responded to pressure from them."

Alana's mouth dropped open. Mac said, "Well, I'll be goll damned."

Trent swung the rope again, cued Baylor to canter and off they went. He was weak. No doubt about that. Already he could feel the tops of his thighs burning, and his rear. Hell, it was *all* sore.

But his lower legs. They were working! He might not be able to feel them, but Baylor sure could.

"Here come the steers," Mac called out.

Trent kept on cantering, swinging his rope, his heart pounding. He urged Baylor to go faster. The horse responded. In seconds he was at the end of the arena, Saedra calling out to him, "Look at you go!"

The corners of his mouth just about touched his ears his grin was so big. *Yes, look at him go.*

"Hang on a sec," Rana said. "We'll get some steers loaded up for you."

Steers.

The true test. It was one thing to lope around like a pleasure rider, quite another to hang on while a horse shot out from a chute.

Could he do it?

Alana's eyes were wide, her face nearly as pale as the sand beneath his horse's feet. She clutched the top rail of the fence as if worried she might fall down.

"Ready?" Mac asked, riding up next to him. The big man appeared concerned, too.

"As I'll ever be."

His friend nodded, locked eyes with Saedra, who'd ridden up next to Alana. Rana had tied her horse to the rail and was busy pushing steers down the chute, their cries of protest echoing through the air, her yells of encouragement blending in with the sound.

"What the hell are you doing?"

They all turned. Cabe came storming up to them like a military general about to dress down his troops.

"Alana, what the hell is going on?"

"It's not Alana's fault, Mr. Jensen." Saedra, who was outside the arena, too, jumped off her horse's back, intercepting Cabe. "We all thought it would be a good idea for Trent to try his hand at roping again."

Actually, it'd been Saedra and Alana that'd had had their doubts, but it didn't surprise Trent at all to see Saedra jump to the group's defense.

"As you can see he's handling himself just fine," his best friend added, her hair falling over one shoulder as she quickly turned to face Trent. She gave him a reassuring smile.

Alana's boss didn't appear the least bit reassured by her words.

"I wouldn't give a rat's patoot if he was wearing a tutu and dancing the samba on the back of that horse." He stopped in front of Alana. "You should have run this by me first."

"I know." She held up her hands. "But this could be big for Trent, Cabe. Sooner or later, he has to try." Trent saw her study the ground as she whispered, "He has to believe."

Believe in himself.

That was what she'd said earlier, her desire for him to succeed so great that she'd cast her own fears for his safety aside. Hell, she was willing to stand up to her boss, too, although he'd begun to realize that she looked upon Cabe as more of a brother.

"I don't like it." Cabe shook his head.

"You don't *have* to like it."

Saedra's words caused Cabe's brows to lift. "Excuse me?"

"Oh, for goodness' sake," Saedra cried. "Lighten up and let him try."

"Saedra—"

But Trent's words were interrupted by Alana's touching Cabe's arm. The gesture drew Cabe's attention.

"Stop," she ordered her friend. "I can tell by the look on your face that you're about to say something rude." She glanced at the group in general. "We have guests, Cabe." She gave him a look meant to bring him in line. "I think we should let Trent try." She squeezed her friend's arm, her knuckles blanching from the gesture. "At least once."

Cabe stared at Saedra, the two of them engaged in a silent battle of wills. Trent almost laughed. Cabe would never get his friend to back down. Saedra wasn't that type.

"Once." He glanced at Alana then. "That's it. And if you fall off and injure yourself, Trent, you better not sue me."

Trent hooked his rope around his arm, holding up his hand. "Scout's honor."

But when he turned his horse toward the roping box, the adrenaline pumping through his stomach nearly made him ill. Mac stood in the heeling box to the right. Rana hadn't moved back to her position by the rail, but once she heard her dad give the word, she began pushing steers through the chutes again. Trent busied himself sorting out his rope and reins, Baylor's head lifting when he pointed him toward the ten-by-ten header box.

"Easy."

The horse knew what was coming. If the steers hadn't been a dead giveaway, the twirling rope sealed the deal. But he was a good gelding. He didn't get all hyped up, just calmly walked forward, though his nostrils flared and the muscles in his neck tensed.

"Are these steers fast?" Mac asked Cabe.

"Fast enough."

Competition steers. Corriente, to be exact, skinny little brown-and-white steers with big horns.

"You ready for this?" Mac appeared every bit as anxious as everyone else in the arena. He'd taken off and repositioned his black hat at least ten times. "If you think it's too much—"

"Let's go."

With a final nod, Mac spun his horse around, waiting until the sorrel faced forward before backing him into a corner, although Mac's horse gave him far more trouble than Trent's horse. The animal half reared, and Mac jerked on the reins. When he did it again, Mac said, "Hold on," before circling and trying to settle the sorrel gelding.

Trent tensed.

Mac's horse quieted. The steer in the chute grew quiet, too. Rana, who stood off the back of the metal device, met his gaze. Trent inched his hands closer to Baylor's mane—just in case he needed to hold on.

He nodded.

Rana swung the release.

There was no barrier to break, but Baylor would have come close if there had been one. The big animal shot forward and nearly unseated Trent, who had to clutch mane to keep from falling off.

"Trent!" he heard someone cry.

But it was okay. He regained his balance quickly, had already started to swing his rope, all sound fading away as he homed in on the steer running next to him. He saw everything so clearly in that instant. The hoofprints in the sand.

The quarter-size spot on the steer's rear end. The arena fence shooting by on his left. One twirl, two. On the third he tossed.

And caught.

He almost blew it. Almost forgot to turn and dally, but Baylor knew the drill. The big bay animal leaned to the left, nearly unseating Trent again. Somehow he managed to hang on, to wrap the rope around the horn, Mac coming up behind him, the whiz-whiz-whiz of his twirling rope filling the air just before he, too, tossed.

And caught.

The horse he rode felt the tug on the saddle, slammed on the brakes, spun to face the steer, Trent clutching mane yet again, but he was laughing, and, yes, damn it, his eyes burned, but he didn't care. He just didn't care.

"By God," Mac said, the calf stretched between them before Mac nudged his horse forward and undallied his rope. "We did it."

By God, they had.

Chapter Nineteen

She was ecstatic. Elated. Thrilled.

Alana turned away from the rail. Deflated, sad and worried, too.

"He did it!"

Saedra's cry was one of pure joy, but the words were a stab to Alana's heart. Yes, he'd done it. Done it well. There could be little doubt that even with the damage done to his legs, he could rope again, at the very least.

Saedra jumped in front of her, startling her. "God bless you, Alana McClintock. I don't know how you got him back on a horse, but God bless you." She clutched her shoulders and shook them.

"I didn't do it." She swallowed over the fear she felt. "*He* did it. He believed."

Saedra didn't have time to reply because Cabe stepped between them. "Congratulations."

"Thanks."

Her boss completely ignored Saedra. Mac called for another steer. Less than five minutes later Trent burst out of the chute one more time, although he missed. He didn't seem disappointed, though. His nonstop grin had to be hurting his face. Twice more, he ran, catching both times, but she could tell he was exhausted.

"I'm going to have my work cut out for me." He coiled his

rope before hanging it over his horn. "I feel like I haven't ridden in years."

They were all standing around the rail, everyone but Cabe. Her boss had gone back to his cave after watching Trent catch a second time.

"It'll come back to you," Saedra said. "Just give it some time."

But maybe it wouldn't come back to him, Alana thought. Maybe her fears were all for nothing. Maybe this was as good as he would get.

Shame on you for letting that cheer you up.

"One day at a time," she heard herself say, although once again she spoke to herself more than the group at large.

Saedra turned away from the rail to smile in her direction. "Did you talk to your boss about letting us stay here a night or two?"

"No."

It had seemed to Alana that Cabe couldn't wait to leave the arena, because he'd shot back to his office like a squirrel to his hole. Clearly, her friend didn't feel the need to socialize with their guests, or one guest in particular. She couldn't believe how rude he'd been to Saedra earlier, too.

"I'd like to fix dinner for you guys." Saedra glanced at Mac and Trent. "I make the best barbecue ribs in Colorado."

Mac rubbed his belly. "Seriously. She does."

"I had my own catering business for years. Sold it just two months ago." Saedra glanced at her watch. "There's still time for me to put my horse away, run to the store and come back in time to cook."

Cabe wouldn't say no to that…would he? Honestly, she had a feeling he would, although for the life of her she couldn't understand why he'd taken such an instant dislike to the woman.

"I'm sure he'd love that," Alana lied. "There's a couple empty stalls at the end of the barn. Feel free to put your horses in there."

And that was that.

WITH HIS STOMACH FULL and good friends surrounding a camp-fire off the Jensens' back porch, Trent couldn't remember ever feeling any happier.

"Bet we could be ready to compete in time for Cowboy Christmas."

Cowboy Christmas. Fourth of July weekend. A time when it seemed that every city in every state had a rodeo of some kind. A weekend to make money, if you had the ability to travel.

"I don't know," he said thoughtfully, checking his white shirt for any blobs of barbecue sauce. They'd just finished eating Saedra's famous firehouse ribs, the scent of barbecue still hanging in the air, although they'd eaten without Cabe. Alana's friend had professed he needed to prep for some new guests arriving tomorrow, although Trent had a feeling that had been a lie, especially after spying the way Alana and Rana had looked at each other with lifted brows.

"We could hit three or four rodeos that weekend alone," Mac mused.

The sun had long since sunk below the horizon, so there was no cowboy hat on his head. He missed its presence, though, because the brim was good for hiding surreptitious glances at people. Instead, he was forced to stare outright at Alana, shadows dancing across her skin as the flames from the fire pit between them sporadically flared to life.

"What do you think?" he asked her. "Think I could be ready for that?"

She'd been quiet all evening, so he wasn't surprised when all she did was shrug her shoulders.

"I think you totally could," Rana offered, her gaze fixed on the metal rod she held, or more specifically, the marshmallow on the end of it. "I can't believe how well you did today. You made Baylor look like a competition rope horse."

Alana sat in her lodge pole chair, one with Western stars decorating the back and arms. They all sat in matching seats, all except him. He was still too weak to get up and down com-fortably, so he used his wheelchair, but he didn't mind it so much anymore. He leaned forward and clasped his hands on his lap as he waited—no, hoped—for Alana to answer.

"It sure would be good to see you back in action," Saedra said. "We could all practice again tomorrow."

Why wouldn't she look at him?

"Yeah, sure," he said distractedly.

Saedra had declared they would stay in Mac's horse trailer with the living quarters in the front, although he wasn't certain Cabe had liked the idea. There appeared to be some tension between Cabe and Saedra.

"Heck, Trent," Saedra was saying. "If you keep this up, you might even make it back to the NFR."

The NFR?

His gaze shot to Saedra's. "You think?"

"I do," she said with a nod.

He'd be lying if he didn't admit to the pinpricks of excitement her words stirred in his stomach. Was it possible? His old rope horse, Dee, was back at home in Colorado, but he'd be back there soon.

Colorado. No Alana.

His gaze sought hers out again. She stared into the flames, her black hair having been set loose at some point so that it flowed down the front of her shoulders, firelight staining it red in places, her black eyelashes seeming to be outlined in soot. There was so much elegance to her looks. She was the type of woman who would only grow more beautiful with age.

"I think it's a little early to be talking about the NFR."

The words came from Alana, the first ones she'd spoken in nearly an hour.

"I think anything is possible," he countered back.

They stared into each other's eyes, but then she suddenly shot up. "I'm going to retire for the evening."

He reared back in his chair. "No. Don't go." He wasn't trying to contradict her, he just felt Saedra was right, maybe he could do it. Heck, she was the one to encourage him to *believe*.

"I'm tired," she said quickly. "Saedra, thanks for a delicious meal. Those were the best ribs I've ever had."

"But you haven't had any marshmallows yet," Rana complained.

"Later, kiddo." She came up behind the teenager, rested her hands on her shoulders and squeezed gently. "I'll see you in the morning."

She didn't meet his gaze again, didn't so much as look in his direction. He couldn't keep his gaze off her as she melted away from the firelight. She didn't have far to go, he noticed. The campfire was bright enough to illuminate a pathway off the back of the house, one that led to a single-story dwelling of some sort. He watched her disappear inside.

"You going to go after her?"

Saedra spoke the words, though they caused Rana to lift her head, but only for a moment. Her marshmallow had started to smoke, the smell of burnt sugar filling the air; the end of it suddenly caught on fire.

"Darn," he heard her mutter.

"No, I'm not going after her," he said softly, silently adding *not yet* to the end of his sentence.

"Go after who?" Rana asked before taking a big bit of her marshmallow, eyes curious. "Alana?"

Clearly, the teenager had no clue what was going on between them. That was good. He didn't need youthful romanticism compounding the issue.

"Not Alana," Trent said. "She meant if I was going to retire for the evening, too, like Alana." Trent shot Saedra a look of reproach. "But I was hoping you could answer a question before I turn in for the night."

The girl took another bite of her marshmallow, a bit of the gooey insides dribbling down her chin, which caused her to grin in a silly fashion before she swiped it away.

"Sure." But the word came out sounding like *shush,* thanks to her full mouth.

"Do you think Alana would take a job if an offer came in from the Professional Rodeo Cowboys Association?"

Rana stopped chewing, but only for a moment. "You mean, like, a full-time deal?" She frowned. "Leave the ranch and everything?"

Trent nodded.

She blinked, saying a split second later, "Never." She swallowed the rest of her treat.

"What if she met someone?" Saedra asked. Mac stared between two of them curiously.

Rana did the same thing, her eyes darting from Mac to Saedra to Trent then back again before saying, "You guys want to set her up with someone or something?"

Trent almost laughed. Saedra caught his eye, smiled, then said, "Something like that."

"Someone on the rodeo circuit?"

"That's the general idea," Saedra replied.

"Who?"

Saedra just shook her head. "Never mind that. It won't matter if she refuses to leave the ranch."

But Rana was already shaking her head. "You're right. She won't leave. Wouldn't matter if it was Ty Murray you wanted her to date, although my dad told me he's already married to some singer, but still. Alana hated being out on the road with my uncle." The teenage girl suddenly lost her smile. "That's how come she wasn't with us the night it…" She frowned. "You know, when *it* happened."

The accident.

As if suddenly needing to do something, Rana bent and fished another marshmallow out of the bag near her feet. She pulled out two this time.

"Besides," she added after spearing the two marshmallows, "she can't leave now. My dad is thinking of expanding next year. We'll need her help with that."

"Hmm," Saedra mused.

"But if the guy was local—" Rana's smile was back on her

face "—that would be a different story." She paused. "But I don't think there are any PRCA cowboys around here, at least none that are good enough for Alana."

"I would have to agree," Saedra said. "So I guess that answers that question."

Trent felt the need to move. He rolled his chair back from the fire before he could stop himself. Saedra turned to him, concern shining from her eyes.

"Gonna retire for the evening?" she asked.

"Yup."

"Do you need a ride?" Rana offered. "I can drive you down in the Mule. I'm allowed to do that."

"No, no. I like to stroll through the trees."

"But you won't be able to see."

"I have super vision," he said with a smile, but it was forced. He wouldn't need night vision, since he had no intention of returning to his cabin. He planned to hang out near the barn until everyone went to bed. "I'll be fine."

Saedra must have realized what he meant to do because she stood suddenly. "I'll walk with you."

"I'm going to turn in, too," Mac said with a yawn, lifting his arms over his head. He reminded Trent of a giant toddler.

"All right," Rana said, clearly disappointed.

"Relax. I'm still here for a few more days. We can do this again."

He wheeled himself over to the girl, happy when she leaned forward and gave him a hug. She was a good kid, one who'd go far in college rodeo if she stuck with it.

"You couldn't have picked someone closer to home to dive into a relationship again?" Saedra said the moment they were out of earshot.

"It's not like I had this planned," Trent grumbled.

"What are you going to do?"

"Whatever it takes."

But he would be lying to himself if he didn't feel some apprehension as he approached Alana's apartment later that evening. Saedra and Mac had retired for the night. Rana, too, by the looks of it, although the fire still flared in the sunken fire pit. As luck would have it, Alana's place had a handicap ramp, a remnant of her time spent helping Rana, he assumed. He tried to be quiet as he wheeled himself up the ramp, but his wheels made a steady clack-clack, clack-clack as they passed over wooden slats.

"Alana," he whispered, afraid to raise his voice lest someone hear him inside the big house. "Are you up?"

No answer.

Was she asleep? Or was she purposely trying to avoid him? He knocked lightly just in case she couldn't hear him.

"Alana?" he repeated again, louder.

She wasn't asleep. He didn't know how he knew that, but he did. Clearly, he had his answer about whether or not she would move to Colorado for him. Based on the way she'd behaved this evening, she didn't want to move forward in an actual relationship.

To hell with that.

They'd shared something the evening before. Something rare and remarkable, and he didn't care what her thoughts were on long-term relationships, he wasn't about to walk away.

He tried the door. Locked. "Damn," he muttered under his breath. But then he saw it. One of the windows was open a crack. They were Dutch windows, the type that slid upward, and he didn't hesitate as he wheeled himself forward. Relief flooded him when he managed to pull the screen off with a minimum of effort. The window lifted easily, too, but the problem was how to lift himself over the ledge. While he'd regained some of his strength, he wasn't strong enough to lift his legs up and over the sill.

He peeked inside.

Darkness greeted him. A small coffee table sat under the window, next to a couch, and a lamp with a base shaped like a horse's head sat on the table. In for a penny, in for a pound.

With a Herculean effort he lifted himself onto the sill. He

clasped the frame tightly and then shimmied backward. Thanks to months of wheeling himself around, his upper body was strong enough, but there came a time when gravity took over, and Trent knew his legs would slide inward. With a twist of his hips, first one then the other fell inside. They hit the coffee table. Hard. The lamp fell. He cursed. From the back of the house he heard, "What the—"

But now that he was inside, he didn't know where to go.

He needn't have worried. Five seconds later he was face-to-face with Alana.

Chapter Twenty

"My lamp!"

Trent blinked against the sudden light and stared at her like a child who'd been caught tossing the cat into the bathwater.

"It's okay," he said quickly. "It's not broken."

He sat on the window sill, his eyes wide, and for some strange reason, Alana wanted to cry. Only it wasn't so strange. She knew why. She'd spent the whole evening trying to avoid him. Had realized sometime between his debut at roping and the dinner Saedra had cooked that any relationship with him would be so complicated they shouldn't even bother trying.

"You have to leave."

"No."

"Trent—"

"No." There was a couch next to the table he'd disrupted. He grabbed the arm and lowered himself onto the plush seat. "I'm not leaving. I'll crawl to your bedroom if I have to."

Her heart stopped.

She'd been fighting a battle all evening, one centered around fear. Fear of him leaving. Fear of him breaking her heart. Fear of him returning to the rodeo circuit and finding someone who would worship the ground he walked upon, someone who'd follow him to the ends of the earth, someone who didn't mind the long hours, the days away from home or living out of a trailer...

Not someone who couldn't bear the thought of leaving

Rana—the girl she loved like a daughter—even for a little while.

"I can't." But once again, she was speaking more to herself than anyone else. "I just can't."

He shifted, wrenched himself upward, and then he was standing. "You going to make me walk to you?"

"Trent, no."

He swung his hips and his left leg moved. He almost fell, corrected himself at the last minute.

"Let me help you.'

"No." He held out a hand. "I'm going to do this, Alana. For you."

Suddenly, she was close to tears. Of all the moments to have a breakthrough…to pass from merely standing to walking, actually *walking*.

He took another step.

She closed her eyes, but only for a second, because she wanted him to succeed, would catch him if he fell, her heart ramming her chest with every footfall.

"I would walk to the ends of the earth for you, Alana."

Heat stained her cheeks. Tears, she realized. Would he? Would he give it all up for her? Stay by her side here on the ranch? Would he do that for her? Did she even have a right to ask?

"Haven't you guessed?" he said softly. "I've never felt this way before."

No, she immediately countered. It was all an illusion. Some type of twisted Florence Nightingale thing. He didn't have any feelings for her, not *real* feelings. It was just sexual attraction. She felt it, too. Criminy, she couldn't even look at the man without her insides melting. Couldn't touch him without wanting to caress him more. Couldn't be near him without wanting to get closer.

"Trent."

He was right in front of her now, wobbly, but only an arm's length away.

"Let me hold you tonight."

She almost laughed. Hold her? There would be no holding. She knew the moment his skin made contact with her own they would be lost. Once again she told herself to step back, out of range, but her feet refused to move, and then his hand lifted; his fingers found her cheek. She told herself not to move, but she tilted her head toward him nonetheless. Her eyes closed, and she knew, she knew it was all over.

A split second later, she sensed the heat of his body, knew he'd closed the distance. She felt his breath on her face. His shirt smelled of smoke and marshmallows and that cinnamon-like scent that was Trent.

"Let me make love to you."

He kissed her. Her whole body ignited. Just one touch and she was gone.

Trent. Oh, Trent. Don't you know what you do to me?

But she couldn't say the words out loud, couldn't do much more than groan as his tongue slipped between her lips, finding the heat in her mouth and igniting a different sort of heat between her thighs.

He leaned into her. It took her a moment to realize that he was asking her to move. She scooted backward, toward her bed on the opposite wall. The back of her knees hit first. She sank down, stared up at him. This man, this amazing man, he'd gone through so much and yet had managed to come out on the other side. The similarities in their backgrounds was like a bonding agent. She understood him. Admired his fortitude. Couldn't be happier for him. As he stood over her, he reminded her of the old Trent, the one she'd seen on TV, the man who wouldn't take no for an answer, and that gave new meaning to the word *try.*

She loved his try.

"Do you have any idea what you do to me when you look at me like that?"

Yes. She experienced the same shivers of excitement when he stared down at her, too. Trent. Her rodeo star. Someone she shouldn't be crossing the line with—patient and therapist—yet she found herself slowly stripping despite telling herself not to. He did the same, the dim glow coming from her bathroom shedding light into her bedroom. Her jeans came off next, then her bra and underwear. He had stripped down, too, though she couldn't recall watching him do so. They were skin to skin so quickly it took her breath away.

"Alana," he sighed as they collapsed onto the bed.

They kissed again, more harshly, more deeply than before, his tongue sliding deep into her mouth and causing her to groan because she wanted more. She wanted the heat. She wanted *him*.

His mouth slipped away. He met her gaze, the intensity in his eyes causing her insides to spasm, but then he ducked to the side so he could kiss her neck. She shivered. He nipped her collarbone. She arched into him because she knew where he was headed, knew what he wanted to do. When his tongue found her breast she cried out in pleasure. His tongue flicked out. Her nipple contracted so quickly she moaned of pleasure all over again, the sight of him kissing her causing more spasms of delight to ripple through her body.

Something brushed her center. His hand, she realized, as her legs fell open of their own accord. His fingers teased her with the same precision as his tongue and she knew, she just knew, she would climax soon. It was the forbidden fruit. A temptation to sin. The superstar she'd admired from afar. And she wanted him—*bad*.

"Please," she ordered, squirming beneath him.

She felt him shift and he was there, right there, the tip of him poised over her center.

He plunged.

They both cried out.

He took her this time, possessed her as only a man who wanted a woman badly could, his hips lifting and thrusting and causing such intense contractions of pleasure, such a perfect mix of lust and longing, that she wrapped her legs around his backside and demanded more.

"Alana," he cried before kissing her again, more harshly, more deeply than before.

She lost her sense of self, her ability to think. They moved as one, his flesh melting into her flesh, his fingers twining together with her fingers, his heart matching the rhythm of her own.

And then…and then…fire. And ice. And feelings so intense she cried out his name in surprise.

He didn't stop.

He wouldn't let her wallow. Oh, no, he kept teasing and thrusting and moving so that she climbed again, higher this time, her moans matching his moans until once again he brought her there, right there, and Alana fell off the cliff all over again.

He collapsed. She held him. They were all sweat and tangled limbs and ragged breaths.

"You amaze me," she heard him say.

He lifted his head at the same time his hands found her hair, brushing it back from her face, his pupils dark with spent passion. "I can't imagine being apart from you."

He brushed more hair off her face while everything inside Alana stilled, but only for a second, because her pulse began racing all over again at the look upon his handsome face.

Tenderness. Amazement. *Joy.*

She started to cry because this was all wrong on so many levels.

He pulled her to him tight, and he must have thought she cried out of happiness because he kissed the top of her head gently, tenderly, but that wasn't why she cried at all. She cried because she knew, she just *knew* things could only end in heartache. In a little over a week he would leave, and he would expect her to go with him, or to follow him on the rodeo circuit, or to end up in Colorado, and that was a life she couldn't face.

Not again. Not when she'd worked so hard to remake her own life after Braden's passing.

"Let me stay with you tonight," he asked.

But what about for a night? One more evening. There was nothing wrong with that.

He kissed her lips and she was lost. Again. Although maybe she wanted to be lost. Maybe she wanted to be selfish, to have him one last time, to imagine them together like this, here on the ranch…forever.

She pulled her lips away. "Hold me."

"I will," he said between kisses. "I'll hold you all night."

And he did.

SHE'D SNUCK OUT of bed again.

"Damn it," Trent said, sitting up, only to gasp.

Pain.

It radiated down his legs. For a moment he forgot his irritation as he marveled at the myriad of sensations that flowed up and down his legs. Not just his thighs.

His calves, too. Pain. Tenderness. Taut muscles. As if someone had flipped a switch the receptors in his brain had turned back on.

"Holy—"

He pulled the covers back to examine his legs. Scars still crisscrossed the surface, his calves were still much smaller than they had been, but when he reached out and ran a finger down his leg, he felt the tiny hairs that dotted his skin stir, goose bumps sprouting where his fingers had been.

"Well, I'll be…"

Where was Alana?"

He spotted the note then, off to his right, on a nightstand.

Trent,
I'm off to the airport to fetch some guests. I'll be busy all day. There's fresh coffee in the kitchen. Enjoy.

That was it. No *Love, Alana*. No *I'll miss you*. No nothing.

He told himself to settle down. After last night could there be any doubt that Alana cared for him? They'd spent hours in each other's arms, and though they had done very little talking, who needed words for what they had?

Through sheer force of will he grunted and groaned his way through finding his clothes, and then, using the walls and furniture, he slowly and painfully recovered his wheelchair. Thankfully, her place was handicap equipped, and a soak in the hot tub soothed him.

He was just getting dressed when he heard someone call out, "Trent? You in there?"

Saedra.

"Come on in," he said, snapping the last button on his shirt as he sat in his chair. "I'm in the back. In the bathroom."

She found him an instant later. "My, my, my," she said, her eyes scanning him sitting in his chair, steam still wafting through the air. "You look like you're right at home."

"Had to take a bath." He shook his head ruefully. "I'm so sore I can barely move."

Saedra's eyes widened. "Sore? As in you can feel things?"

"All the way to my toes."

"Trent! That's great."

"I know. I just wish Alana was here so I could tell her."

As if noticing her absence, Saedra looked around. "Where is she?"

"Fetching guests from the airport." He tucked the end of his shirt in his jeans, groaning.

Saedra laughed. "You need me to find some ibuprofen?"

"I would love that."

"Coming right up."

He'd rolled his way into the family room by the time Saedra emerged from the kitchen, pill bottle in hand.

"You're in luck." She shook the pills before opening the bottle and handing him two.

"Thank You, God."

She settled herself onto Alana's couch, glancing around as she did so. Trent did, too, even though it felt is if he rummaged through Alana's underwear drawer just by being there, a stupid notion given the night they'd just spent together.

"Nice place." Saedra's gaze hooked on a wall of photos opposite the couch. "Small, but quaint."

Trent followed the direction her head was turned. Amidst the twenty or so photos he spotted Cabe and Rana and Alana, some on horseback, some with guests, a few during the holidays. In the middle, however, was a photo that was larger than the others, of Alana laughing up at a man he recognized as Braden.

"Who's that?" Saedra walked up to the same photo he'd spotted. "Looks kind of familiar."

"That's Cabe's brother."

Saedra glanced over at Trent. "She used to date Cabe's brother?"

"No. She was all set to marry Cabe's brother, although they weren't officially engaged."

Her mouth dropped open next. "Wait, wait, wait. How'd I miss that?"

Trent explained about Braden's accident. And about Rana and how Cabe had lost his wife in the same accident.

"Wow," she said when he'd finished.

"I guess it was pretty bad."

Saedra's expression told him she figured it probably was.

"Please tell me you're not the first guy she's been with since then."

"Pretty sure I am."

"Oh, jeez."

"What? There's nothing bad about that."

"Are you kidding? A woman doesn't just get over something like that."

"It's been years."

"And she hasn't dated anyone since. Does that not tell you something?"

Put like that, he supposed she had a point.

And that might explain her disappearing acts.

"You think she's not over him?"

"I think there's that possibility."

He swiped a hand over his face. "I asked if she'd move to Colorado for me."

Saedra flung herself back on the couch. "You did *what?*"

"She said maybe."

"And you say she disappeared this morning because she's picking up guests?"

"That's what she said."

"Let's hope she's telling the truth."

"You think she might be trying to avoid me?"

After the night they'd just shared, he silently told himself, it seemed impossible.

"I think you better slow it down, cowboy." Concern shone from Saedra's eyes. "I like Alana, I really do. I think she's amazing, but both of you, you're just getting over these horrible tragedies."

Not for the first time, he wondered if Saedra had been in love with Dustin, because her face changed, a sadness entering her eyes that seemed to be soul deep. Of course, Dustin had been her friend, too, and so it might just be that. Or not.

"Don't worry. I know what I'm doing."

He hoped.

Chapter Twenty-One

She wasn't trying to avoid him, Alana told herself. She had work to do. Chauffeuring their new guests. Showing them to their cabin. Helping them to understand the layout of the ranch. She wasn't trying to avoid Trent. Not at all.

Liar!

She couldn't avoid him forever, though. Intuitively she knew that, just as intuitively she knew the end was near. Though they had spent the night together, she'd never broached the subject of their future. She'd been too scared to do that.

"Where have you been?" he asked the moment she returned to her apartment.

She strove for a breezy tone of voice when she said, "Oh, here and there," and forced a smile to her face.

She held his gaze, searching for something to fill the silence, but of course, what could she say? *Thanks for the good time, but I really think we should stay away from each other from here on out?*

"You okay?" he asked after the silence stretched on.

"Fine," she lied. She glanced at his chair. "How are your legs this morning?"

"Sore." He rubbed the tops of them. He gave her a smile. "That's one of the things I wanted to talk to you about. I'm feeling things in my calves today."

This time, her smile was genuine. "That's great."

"I had to take some ibuprofen."

Under normal circumstances, she would have offered an hour-long massage, but he wasn't a normal guest and the thought of touching him again... She went all red just thinking about it, and thinking about him, and what he'd done to her last night.

"I had to take a bath." He gave her a crooked smile. "Wish you'd been with me."

She looked up, down, around, anywhere but at him. What could she say? There was a part of her that wished she'd been with him, too. But the other part of her—the sane part—urged her to cool it.

They lapsed into silence, Alana wondering how two people who'd done such amazing things with each other could suddenly run out of things to say.

"Walk with me?" He motioned with his chin toward the road, past Cabe's house.

She shouldn't, she really shouldn't. Cabe had asked her to run to town for some supplies, and she'd promised Rana she'd help her dig out her summer clothes....

"For a minute."

She didn't offer to push him along, she knew better than that. He thrust himself toward the pathway that led toward the main road.

"You know, twice now I've woken up without you by my side."

"I know, but both times I had to get up early and I didn't want to wake you."

Liar!

She hadn't wanted to face him. It was as if her courage deserted her the moment morning arrived. This morning she'd rolled over and spied him sleeping next to her and been choked by a sudden surge of fear. He was just so damn good-looking, more so in the morning when a day's growth of beard darkened his chin and sleep relaxed the stress on his face. She'd watched his chest rise and fall, so tempted to run her fingers over his muscles that she'd had to get out of bed just to stop herself.

"Why do I have the feeling that's not entirely true?"

Because you seem to know me so well, it's frightening.

While she struggled to find the words to placate him, she heard him say, "Saedra thinks we're moving too fast."

She stopped, glanced down at him. They had just reached the top of the road, cows moaning in the distance. The sound of it should have soothed her, but she could tell her palms were sweaty and her heart beat too fast.

"What do you think?"

A cricket chirped nearby. Alana found the sound so wildly appropriate that she almost laughed, especially given that Trent didn't answer, at least not at first.

"I'd rather know what you think."

Coward. But, as usual, she spoke to herself.

She took a deep breath, walking forward again, Trent alongside. The scent of dank earth and vegetation filled the air. Years ago, before Braden had died, he and Cabe had worked for weeks clearing the pasture to their right of too many trees, but they were slowly making a comeback, small pines stretching skyward, the scent of their needles filling the air.

"I think maybe she has a point," she said at last, relieved that he hadn't pushed her to answer, had merely waited, his gaze also scanning the scenery.

"I want to keep seeing you."

Why did she suddenly feel like crying? "And I want to keep seeing you, too."

There. She'd said it. As hard as it was to admit, she had feelings for Trent. Feelings that scared the you-know-what out of her. Feelings that she hadn't felt in, well, not since…

She closed her eyes. *Braden.*

Fingers brushed her own. She glanced down in time to see Trent clasp her hand. It made her insides do that weird thing again, caused her heart to go thump-thump.

"Mac thinks I'm good enough to compete at the local level. He was wondering if it'd be okay if I used Baylor, and if we all could use him this weekend. Guess there's a local roping event somewhere nearby."

"I think that'd be great." The breath she released felt as if it'd been pent up for days. "I'll have to check with Cabe, although I'm sure he won't mind." She swallowed, the sensation that she was on the edge of a cliff making her dizzy for a moment.

He squeezed her hand again. "Thanks."

She gathered her courage, looked him in the eye, the softness in his gaze causing her to look away, as if she might cry or something.

You could fall in love with this man.

She took a deep breath, admitting that maybe she could, and that there was nothing wrong with that, right? He was a good soul. A bit damaged, but so was she.

A man who lived in Colorado.

She shushed the ever-present annoying voice of reason. Yes, they might have some issues to work through, but if it was meant to be...

But later that night, as Trent slept beside her, she had the horrible sensation that she'd been kidding herself. That maybe this whole thing was just a diversion, a blip on the map of his recovery that he would later look back upon and regret. That she would regret.

Quiet, she told herself.

Time would tell which direction the wind blew. Until then she needed to stop with the doom and gloom.

Didn't she?

TRENT HAD LITTLE OPPORTUNITY to see Alana over the next three days. She was busy with new guests, the New Horizons Ranch seeming to come alive, all the cabins full by the end of the week. There were other new arrivals, too. Several locals who were employed by Cabe. The place became a hive of activity, and Trent had a whole new appreciation for what Cabe and Alana did on a regular basis.

"You ready for tomorrow?" Mac asked one night after dinner.

Turned out there was a campfire every night in the Jensen backyard. Guests were always invited, sometimes Cabe throwing steaks or whatever they wanted on the barbecue, sometimes the guests just showing up for the experience of being on a ranch and gathering around the flames.

Tonight they had four new arrivals. Alana was talking to a little girl in a wheelchair, her mom and dad deep in conversation to his left. Trent's own wheelchair had been set off to the side. He'd walked to the campfire under his own steam, something that had filled Alana's eyes with pride. As he thought back over the past two weeks, he admitted she'd been right. While his calves would never be the same, it'd turned out a lot of his problems were the result of his own mental issues. Alana had recommended counseling and he'd agreed. She had someone local come in and talk to him, and it had helped. Miraculously, he'd gotten better and better.

"I think I'm ready," he said when he noticed Mac staring at him expectantly. "I'm getting stronger and stronger."

Mac slapped him on the back. It was just the two of them. Saedra was nowhere to be seen. She'd been holed up in the trailer after offering to help Cabe around the ranch and being firmly rebuffed, Cabe citing something about liability. Saedra's nose had been out of joint ever since.

"You looking forward to going home?" Mac asked. "Next week and you'll be on your way."

He nodded. He'd decided to ride home with Saedra and Mac rather than fly, and they'd agreed to hang out with him and wait. Easier that way and why not? He wasn't particularly fond of flying.

"I'm sure your mom will be glad to see you," Mac added.

She would, and he was looking forward to seeing her and to getting back to his old routine. His mom lived with him in Colorado, something that had come in handy over the years while he was on the road. But when he'd spoken to her last night his mom had sensed he wasn't himself. He hadn't told her about Alana, although for the life of him he couldn't figure out why.

She'd mentioned nothing about moving to Colorado.

The thought was like a song stuck in the back of his head. He'd been afraid to ask her about it, wanted to give her more time, but if she said no, he would work around her. He would come back. In a week or two. He'd really like that, but when he'd broached the subject of future visits with her last night she'd brushed him off.

As if sensing his thoughts about her, their gazes met. Trent realized in that moment that he was well on his way to being a goner. She made him feel things, crazy sensations that he'd never felt before. He just had no clue how they were going to make a long-distance relationship work.

Maybe they could split their time between the two ranches? Maybe she'd be willing to do therapy out of Colorado, too. He would need to talk to her about that.

It was an idea that wouldn't go away, and one he raised with her that night. She'd been insistent they keep their relationship a secret, although he suspected Cabe knew. Crap, he'd left his wheelchair on the porch that first night. Still, he'd been forced to wheel himself back to her place later that night, and their lovemaking had been…different. Less intense. More soft, Alana holding him for a long time afterward.

"Do you think you could find work in Colorado?"

He hadn't meant to blurt the words out loud and regretted them the moment they filled the air. Her shoulders went rigid in his arms, her eyes shooting to his own.

"I'm sure I could."

But she didn't want to. He could see it in her eyes.

It's too early, Trent. Slow down.

"Just a thought."

But for the first time, she pulled away from him. And even though he told himself it wasn't because of his words, he knew better.

"You want this to work, don't you?" he heard himself ask.

"I do, Trent, I really do."

"So what's the problem?"

She shifted her gaze away, looking anywhere but at him, a habit of hers when she felt uncomfortable, he realized.

"I just don't know *how*." He thought she might have tears in her eyes. Maybe. "My life is here. Everything I know and love is right here at this ranch."

Including him?

He wanted to ask that, but knew he couldn't. Crap, he wasn't entirely certain he was in love with her yet, either.

Yes, you are.

But he turned away from that, focused on her eyes instead. "I won't be gone all the time."

"I know."

"And you could come visit, couldn't you?"

She nodded.

He smiled. "Then we'll take it from there."

But something about her gaze made him uncertain, made him wonder if she hadn't been nodding as a way to get him to drop the subject.

The next morning he slipped out of bed ahead of her. It was Saturday, her day off, according to Rana, unless she was haranguing him to do therapy. He smiled as he thought back to last weekend—had it only been last weekend? It felt as if he'd known her forever, so much so that he didn't want to leave her. Still, he felt the need to get to the roping arena early so he could warm up and judge for himself if he was capable of competing, so he left Alana alone, kissing her softly on the cheek as she slept.

Early morning light cast a gray sheen over the interior of her bedroom, but it turned her skin the color of ivory, her black hair spilling out around her. She took his breath away, this woman, and he honestly didn't know how he would stand being apart from her.

Maybe I do love her.

They pulled out of New Horizons Ranch less than an hour

later, before Alana woke up, which had been the plan. She and Cabe and Rana would all show up later, and to be honest, Trent was glad. He needed to focus, something that he suspected might be hard to do if Alana were around.

His nerves only increased when he spotted the number of trailers parked outside a massive covered arena nestled in the foothills outside Reno. This was no weekend gathering of local ranchers.

"What is this?" he asked Mac.

"An ACTRA event."

American Cowboy Team Roping Association, some of the toughest ropers in the country. "For Pete's sake, Mac, couldn't you have chosen something a little easier?"

"What the difference?" Saedra asked from the backseat. She had decided to bring her own horse along for the experience, though she wouldn't be roping. "Team roping is team roping no matter if it's at a rodeo or somewhere else."

She made it sound so easy, but Trent knew better. "I don't think Baylor's a good enough horse to be competitive here."

Mac shot him a sideways glance as he navigated his rig around back—the only place there was parking.

"I thought you weren't interested in competing," Mac teased. "That this was supposed to be practice for you."

"Yeah, but I don't want to make a fool of myself."

It was a lie. He knew it the moment he said the words. He didn't want to lose. Baylor might not be Dee, his best head horse back home, but he was a pretty decent sort. As long as Trent's legs held out, he thought he and Mac might have a shot at some prize money.

"You'll be fine," Saedra said.

They unloaded the horses, Mac and Saedra saddling up while Trent looked on from his wheelchair. Mac had handed him a shirt earlier, one that he must have left behind at some point in the past. The thing was beige and covered with the logos of Trent's former sponsors.

Maybe they wouldn't be former in a few months.

He refused to get his hopes up. But his heart launched itself into his throat when it was time to get on board. Baylor was the perfect gentleman. Trent really liked Cabe's horse, so much so that he might see if he could buy the gelding.

"Here we go," Mac said, guiding his horse toward the main road.

A few people did double takes as they rode by, but Trent had himself convinced it was Saedra on board her own horse that drew the eyes. He was proved wrong less than five minutes later when someone called out, "Holy crap, it *is* the two of you."

He glanced at a towheaded kid who rode toward them, the boy's mouth open before he slapped it closed, the rope he'd been twirling suddenly limp by his side.

"Someone said they'd seen you, but I didn't believe them. You two are like—" the kid shook his head, brown eyes shining "—the Tom Brady and Wes Welker of the rodeo circuit."

"Hey, now," Mac teased. "Don't insult us by comparing us to football players."

The kid smiled. "What are you doing here?"

"Roping," Mac said. He glanced toward Trent. "It's his first time out since the wreck."

"Wow." The kid stared at the two of them in awe. "I can't wait to watch."

There wouldn't be much to watch, Trent almost said, but he just smiled at the kid and tried to focus on his horse. It was hard. The boy wasn't the only one. He could hear hushed voices and feel pointed stares as he rode around the crowded arena.

Ignore them.

He focused on his legs. No pain today. Definitely weak, but nothing too bad.

Baylor tossed his head when Trent uncoiled the rope. Cabe had told him the horse had been used for competitions before, but that he didn't have much oomph out of the box, so Cabe had offered the use of his good horse, Jacob. Trent had declined. He didn't want a rocket launcher, he wanted to take it easy today. He had a feeling, though, that Baylor might surprise even Cabe. The horse was amped.

"First round qualifying starts in an hour," Saedra told them from the rail. "You guys are out thirty-fifth."

"How many teams?" Trent asked.

"Over two hundred."

Damn.

He'd heard the series attracted a lot of competition, but the number still amazed him. That was more than professional rodeos.

He was never more glad than when he spotted Alana approaching, a reaction that surprised him. Usually when he dated a woman he liked to keep his distance on competition days, but his initial impulse was to canter Baylor up to her, bend down and plant a kiss on her lips.

"Look at you ride," she said with a smile.

"All thanks to you," he said. Well, her and his new therapist. He pulled Baylor up at the rail, his hat nearly coming off he stopped so hard. He shoved it back down. "Where's Cabe and Rana?"

"Off to find seats."

Which meant they were all alone, Mac and Saedra having headed back to the trailer.

"How do you think you're going to do?"

"Good, I think."

"Legs holding up?"

"Just fine." He patted the tops of his thighs. "A little sore still."

She nodded. "You should expect that."

So sayeth the therapist. "Alana, about last night—"

"Not now." She held up a hand. "I don't want to talk about you leaving. You need to focus—"

"I'd like to fly you out to Colorado next weekend."

"Trent—"

"You need to meet my mom."

"I'll be working."

"Not on Saturday. I could fly you out on Friday. You could be back by Sunday morning. And surely Cabe could spare you for a day or two."

"It's the start of the busy season." She shook her head, her eyes seeming to look anywhere but at him—again. "But you could fly back here and stay with us, if you wanted."

A horse cantered by him, the animal brushing Baylor and causing the gelding to jerk his head up. This was the wrong place and the wrong time to be discussing this, Trent knew, but he couldn't seem to stop himself.

"I suppose I could, but I don't know. There's so much to do, especially if I decide to hit the road again."

Finally, finally, she looked him in the eye. "I know."

"What about the following weekend?"

She shook her head.

Damn it. She had to be free sooner or later.

"Maybe we should talk about this later." She stepped back from the rail.

"Alana—"

"I'm going to go find Cabe and Rana."

"We can walk over together."

"No." She lifted her chin. "You stay here. Warm up. You need to do that." He saw her take a deep breath, saw her wrestle a smile to her face. "Good luck today, Trent."

"Thanks."

He watched her walk away, but as he did so, he couldn't shake the feeling that she was wishing him good luck about something else. Like good luck in life.

Chapter Twenty-Two

She'd never been more conflicted.

What were they going to do? she wondered, crossing her arms in front of her as she walked toward the massive covered arena. She couldn't leave Rana and the ranch, especially not now during the start of their busy season, but she knew that was what Trent wanted. Maybe not at first. At first he might be content with a weekend here or there, but then what? If things became more serious he would expect more. He had a right to expect more—but could she give it to him?

She shoved the thought away, finding Cabe and Rana a short while later, the two of them waving to her in greeting before she sat down between them. She became almost oblivious to what went on. Team after team ran after steers, some of them catching, some of them not. When Trent and Mac arrived, she told herself she didn't care how they did, but it was a lie. She wanted Trent to do well, even if by doing so it took him further away—that was the problem.

She'd known it might come down to this. They were two different people with two very successful careers. That meant a compromise, but she refused to upend her life, and she knew he didn't want to move to California, and that meant a long-distance relationship that she knew in her heart of hearts would never work. It wouldn't be enough to see him here and there. Relationships were tough enough without adding that into the mix.

You should at least give it a try.

Why? she asked herself. Why, when she knew how it would end? Their two different lives. Two different careers. Two different locations.

The crowd cheered.

She looked up in time to realize Trent and Mac had caught, their time one of the fastest yet.

"I'll be damned," she heard Cabe say. "I never would have thought Baylor could be that quick out of the box."

"That's what happens when a professional rides him," Rana quipped.

"Ouch." Cabe smiled in Alana's direction. "I think I've just been insulted."

But her friend's smile faded. "What's wrong?"

Rana turned to face her, too. "Alana, you look like you're about to cry."

Was she? "I'm okay," she lied. "I'm just happy for Trent." And she was. Overjoyed. He deserved a happily ever after.

So when, a couple hours later, Trent and Mac came back for the semifinals, she cheered. The arena had been lit by a plethora of fluorescent lights, but it could have been almost dark and she still would have known Trent was the best header she'd ever seen. He rode against others of similar skill level, the event using a handicap system that ensured everyone had a fair shot, but it didn't matter. The man was poetry in motion. Somehow he squeezed every ounce of speed out of Baylor, the horse breaking so fast Alana was surprised Trent's cowboy hat didn't fly off. Somehow, Trent read the steer so well, the poor animal didn't stand a chance. Trent was right on top of it when it left the chute. And somehow Trent hung on, though she knew his legs had to be killing him, and that it couldn't have been easy working with a horse with far less experience than Trent was used to—but he did it. When he and Mac caught, it didn't surprise her to see them atop the leaderboard.

"Unbelievable," Rana cried, standing up and cheering. "Go, Trent! Go, Mac!"

She would have thought they were too far away to hear,

but Alana saw Trent turn, saw his glaze slide over the crowd, finding her. She smiled, gave him a thumbs-up, and it hit her then how much she would miss him. Such a good man. Kind. Thoughtful. Caring. Yeah, they'd started out on rocky ground, but she'd understood his anger, and now she knew the real Trent Anderson.

"You like him, don't you?"

The words brushed her ear, and Rana had a smile older than her years on her face.

"He's a good guy," Alana hedged.

Rana's smile faded, but only a little. "You should let him know."

"Know what?"

"That you like him."

"Rana, stop."

"Are you afraid?"

"Seriously, Rana, stop. You sound like your dad."

Rana nodded, looked away. They watched a few more teams, but a moment later Rana reached over and clasped her hand. "I love you, Aunt Alana."

Alana felt her breath catch. It was so rare for Rana to call her that. Usually it was for private moments when it was just the two of them.

"I love you, too, kiddo."

She held her gaze. "It's okay if you leave."

Alana straightened sharply, had to work for a moment to squeeze air into her lungs. She forced herself to look into the teenager's gaze. "I'm *not* leaving you, if that's where you're going with that."

"But it would be okay."

No, it wouldn't. She could see the fear in Rana's eyes. Cabe was good with the girl, but for all that he was a wonderful father, he was still a man, still a little too gruff, still suffering from his own sense of loss, yes, even after all this time.

"I'm not leaving you," she said again, more firmly.

Rana smiled.

Trent and Mac ended up winning the event.

She wasn't surprised. Clearly Trent was on his way to a full recovery. Just as clearly he belonged back on the rodeo circuit.

Someone must have tipped off the press, because when she arrived back at the trailer, a camera crew stood there and a pretty blonde reporter was talking to Trent and Mac. They stood in shadow, but a light shone on their faces. Trent sat back in his chair, probably exhausted, and Mac stood beside him. Saedra waved and smiled while stripping the saddle from Baylor's back. She watched the interview, saw how Trent was completely at ease in front of the camera.

And why wouldn't he be?

She'd watched him on national television more times than she could count on one hand. To be honest it seemed surreal to be watching him now, live, answering questions about the horse he rode, his injuries, how he felt about winning, all the while knowing that the hands raised in excitement had touched her own, the lips forming words had covered her mouth, the eyes that shifted in her direction stared not into the camera, but into her own.

For all the wrong reasons.

He'd been lonely. Terrified. She'd been willing and a comfort to his wounded soul. That wasn't exactly the best way to start a relationship.

"Thanks so much," she heard the broadcaster say. "Good luck, Trent. It's great to see you back on your feet."

Mac wasted no time pulling the reporter off to the side, his flirtatious gaze leaving no doubt which way the wind blew. Trent never looked away. Alana forced her feet to move forward.

"Congratulations," she said softly, staring down at him.

He held out his hand. She clutched it, not surprised when he pulled her to him. Alana smelled sweat and cinnamon and all things Trent as she slowly wrapped her arms about him.

"Can you believe it?" she heard him ask.

"Yes." She straightened again, such a mix of emotion filling her up it was all she could do not to cry. Joy. Sorrow. Despair. "I knew you could do it. I always knew."

He still held her hand, squeezed it, Alana squeezing back.

"So, did you ask her?"

Both of them turned. Mac stood there, his gaze darting between the two of them.

"No, Mac, I haven't."

"Asked me what?"

Trent had looked away, and that more than anything alerted her to what was coming.

"We were thinking of leaving for Colorado tonight," Mac announced, "and wondered if you wanted to come along."

"Mac—"

The frustration in Trent's voice was evident. Mac covered his mouth before lifting his hands. "Oops. Guess I wasn't supposed to say anything."

"Tonight?" Alana asked, shocked.

"After we drop off Baylor. Mac says if we drive all night we can make it back in time for another big roping near our hometown."

Tonight. Not next week? Not in a few days?

So much easier.

"You should come," Saedra called, slipping a halter over Baylor's head. "You could meet Trent's mom."

"I—"

"She can't leave." The words came from Cabe who walked toward them. "We have guests arriving next week."

"Surely you could live without her for a day or two?"

It was Saedra who'd spoken, and Alana watched as her friend's easygoing nature suddenly evaporated.

"Working at the ranch is her *job*."

"Dad," Rana said, touching his arm.

The shadows on the ground were as dark as Cabe's eyes. "We need her at the ranch," he said more softly. "Alana knows that."

The knot building in her stomach suddenly doubled in size. "I can't," she said softly. "You know I can't."

Trent had known. She'd told him as much earlier, but that hadn't stopped him from wanting to leave. The breath she'd been taking froze in her chest as she waited for him to say he wouldn't go, that he'd rather stay with her, but instead he released her hand.

He knew their brief romance was over, too.

"We can hook up in a week or so."

No, they wouldn't. This wasn't real—whatever this was— it *couldn't* be real. She'd had a crush on him. She could admit that now. Had watched him for so many years on television always wondering… That was why she'd jumped into bed with him. But now it was over. He was going home. She'd always known he'd eventually go home.

"If you want," she said softly, "I'm sure we can find someone to haul Baylor home. You could leave right now."

"Good idea," Cabe said.

"Yeah, that'd be great," Saedra echoed.

Some of the fire had faded in his eyes. "But my things."

"I can pack them up for you. Send them to your ranch."

She would let him go now. Start on forgetting him.

If you can forget him, a little voice nagged.

"That would work."

For some reason her shoulders fell. She tried to prop them back up, but they refused to move. He'd made his choice. She had made hers. Nothing more left to say.

"Let's do it!" Mac said.

She couldn't look Trent in the eyes. Cabe drifted off to find someone to haul Baylor home, but not before she heard Trent thank him profusely, the two of them shaking hands. Rana came up next to her, the girl sensing something was amiss, her face a mask of concern.

It made her want to cry.

Ten minutes later all was settled. Cabe came and took Baylor off their hands. Rana gave everyone a hug goodbye, Mac loaded up his horse, Saedra loaded hers, too, and soon it was just the two of them, the sound of truck engines roaring to life all around as people prepared to leave the show grounds.

"I guess this is it," she said. She would not cry. She just wouldn't.

"I'll give you a call from the road."

She took a deep breath. "Okay."

He opened his arms. She took another deep breath before she bent down, slipping into his embrace as easily as she had all week, only this was different.

"Thank you," he whispered in her ear.

"You're welcome." She kissed him on the cheek before pulling away, although he tried to hold her to him. She drew back, saying, "Drive carefully."

His gaze searched her own, something he saw in her eyes prompting him to say, "Alana?"

Do not cry.

"Goodbye, Trent." She forced herself to walk away.

"Damn it," Trent muttered, flipping his cell phone closed and tossing it on the couch next to him. "What the hell?"

"Still no answer?" his mother asked from the armchair to his left where she'd been reading, her blue eyes flicking up from her book and connecting with his.

"Nope."

It'd been three days since he left California, and no matter how many times he called, no matter how many messages he'd left, Alana never returned his calls. Oh, his phone had been ringing. Off the hook. But for all the wrong reasons. His interview from last weekend had made national news. Suddenly he was a big headline. Man Makes It Back from Tragic Wreck. He'd become a household name overnight.

"It's like she's trying to avoid me or something."

They were in the family room of his single-story ranch house, a place that reflected his mother's taste in Western decor, although he'd put his foot down when she'd wanted to paint the walls of the kitchen mauve.

"Honey, I think it's time you realized she may not want to hear from you again.

"No way." He shook his head so hard he almost knocked his hat askew. "Impossible."

His mother hadn't aged over the years, not even a little bit. Sure, her long blond hair held streaks of gray now, but her face was as unlined as it'd been the day his father died twenty years ago. How she'd held it together he had no idea, but he couldn't imagine life without her and he trusted her opinion more than he trusted his own—which was why her words sent such a shiver of fear down his spine.

"I know you're head over heels for her, but did you ever consider she might not feel the same way?"

"What makes you think I'm head over heels?"

"Honey, you haven't stopped talking about her since you came home. Of course you're in love her."

Was he?

He straightened suddenly. Damn. He was.

"She loves me, too."

Didn't she?

His mom laughed.

"Son," she said. "Sometimes I worry about the size of your ego."

"Excuse me?"

She set her book down. "She was probably just using you for sex."

"Mom!"

"Well, why not? *Men* do it all the time."

"*I* don't."

She smirked. "Haven't you?"

Beneath the collar of his denim shirt, his neck flushed. "I'm not like that, Mom. You know that."

"Maybe *she* is."

No, he told himself. No way. He'd seen the softness in her

eyes. There could be no mistaking that she had feelings for him. None at all.

"I'm gonna go see her."

His mother's brows lifted. "When?"

He pulled his wheelchair closer to him. He was still weak. That roping last weekend had nearly killed him. He couldn't remember a time when he'd been so sore. But sore was good. Sore meant he could feel something.

"This weekend." He could use his legs well enough that he no longer needed to hoist his lower body into the chair. "That little girl I was telling you about, Rana, she's competing at a high school rodeo. I'm going to fly in and surprise them."

That way she couldn't avoid him.

He hated how insidious the thought was. How, once mentioned, he couldn't get his mother's words out of his mind.

Had she been using him?

That night, as he rode one of his old rope horses around his family's five-hundred-acre ranch checking fences and the condition of his cattle, he replayed their meetings in his mind. Sure, she might not have said she loved him, but that didn't mean anything. He knew in his heart she did.

He flew in on a Saturday morning after checking the California High School Rodeo Association's website for the location. And, as luck would have it, she was riding in Reno, at the same damn rodeo grounds he'd been at with Alana. Coincidence? Or fate?

One thing was for sure, it felt amazing to be able to make the trip on his own two feet, although his wheelchair was safely stowed in the back of his dark blue rental car just in case he needed it.

He arrived just before the rodeo started, just as he had planned, although he'd fretted the whole way there that he'd be too late. The Jensen family had already arrived and as Trent pulled in his second fear assailed him. What if Alana had stayed home?

Then he spotted her, standing by a trailer parked next to

a fence, her long dark hair turning silver in the sunlight. She was smiling up at Cabe, laughing at something he said. Behind them Rana groomed her horse, but the girl must have felt his gaze because she glanced up, her whole face lighting up when she saw it was him.

"Trent!"

His gaze returned to Alana. She stiffened. And Trent knew, he knew the moment he spied the dismay on her face, that his mom had been right.

She *didn't* love him.

Chapter Twenty-Three

What was he doing here?

"You came to watch me ride!" Rana cried out from behind her.

"I'll be damned," Cabe muttered.

"I can't…" Alana's heart felt ready to high-jump out of her chest. "I need…" She swallowed in an effort to lubricate her suddenly dry throat. "I have to go back to the truck for something."

"Alana, what's wrong?" Cabe clutched her shoulders, such concern on his face, and such surprise, she told herself to calm down. "You look like you've seen a gh—" He straightened suddenly, his gaze moving to Trent. "What's going on between the two of you?"

Had he really not known?

"Nothing." She sucked in a deep breath. "I just need to go to the bathroom."

She turned away before Cabe could say another word.

"Alana!"

But it wasn't Cabe who called her back, it was Trent. She didn't look back, didn't want to know if he stopped for a moment to greet Cabe and Rana. She walked faster.

It wasn't fast enough.

"Alana, don't make me chase you."

She stopped suddenly because it was silly to try to flee. He hadn't flown all the way from Colorado to give up on seeing her. She could run, but she couldn't hide.

"Why haven't you called me?" he asked the moment she faced him.

"I…"

What could she say? That she hadn't wanted to talk to him. That she'd been afraid if she'd heard his voice on the phone she would have done anything he asked of her—like jump on a plane to go see him for a night. From there it'd be watching him compete. And from there it'd be move to Colorado. After that it'd be give up her career, and she couldn't, she just wouldn't.

And then there was Rana. She could never abandon her.

"Alana?"

She swallowed again. "I thought it'd be easier."

"Easier how?"

She didn't want to answer. Didn't want to hurt him. And she would. She knew she would.

"To just let things…" She searched for the right word. "Be."

The words hurt him. She could see that in his eyes.

"I love you."

The words knocked the breath out of her. Did he? Or was he in love with the woman who'd helped him walk again?

"Thank you for coming. You just made Rana's day. Probably her whole year."

"*That's* all you've got to say?" He stood there—actually stood there—and it was a miracle, one she'd helped create. The man walked again. "I tell you I'm in love with you and that's all?" He shook his head. "Thanks for coming?"

She shrugged her shoulders. "What do you want me to say?"

"That you love me, too."

She did love him. The moment she'd spotted him standing behind her she'd known it, had felt such a throat-clogging sense of panic, that she'd known. Somehow, crazily, she'd fallen for him.

"Trent," she said softly, almost telling him, changing her

mind at the last minute. It nearly killed her to watch how his face crumbled when she didn't repeat the words.

"So what was it then?" he asked. "Back at the ranch? A fling?"

"No." She looked away, at the ground, the grandstands in the distance, back up at him again. "Maybe at first, but not later."

His face softened. "So what's the problem?"

A million times she'd gone over this conversation, knowing as she did that sooner or later she'd have to come clean.

"I care for you, Trent." She swallowed, hard. "So very, very much. But my life is at the ranch. It's everything to me. Rana..." She shook her head. "She's like a daughter to me. I can't leave her. She's right at that age where she needs me the most."

"You're not her mom."

"No. I could never be Kimberly, but I can be a close second."

"Is it Cabe?" He searched her eyes. "Do you have feelings for him?"

"No," she said sharply. "How could you ask that after everything we've done?"

He reached for her. "Because I just don't understand."

She stepped back. Damn it, she felt tears building behind her eyes. "Please understand, this is as hard for me as it for you."

"Bullshit."

"Goodbye, Trent." She tipped up on her toes and kissed him on the cheek.

He jerked her to him, kissed her on the mouth, hard. She tried to wrench away. He wouldn't let her. It was as if he willed every ounce of his resolve into that kiss, as if he hoped to impose his will onto her own, to somehow convince her without words how much he loved her.

She twisted away.

He stood there, breathing hard, and God help her, she could see the confusion in his eyes. Knew in that instant that he'd finally gotten the message.

"Good luck making it to the NFR."

She had no idea where he went. Didn't know if, in fact, he'd left, or if he'd decided to stick around and watch Rana ride. What she did was apologize to everyone before closing herself off in the living quarters of Cabe's trailer, pleading a blinding headache and the need for peace and quiet. Cabe and Rana had stared at her oddly, but they'd left her alone.

Stupid. You knew this was coming.

And she had, but that didn't make it any easier. The look in his eyes, she thought. The desperation in them. The way he'd kissed her—

She began to weep. Stupid, ridiculous vacation romance. That was all this was, she tried to convince herself. They didn't really love each other.

Then why do you feel so guilty? And why the hell have you been bawling your eyes out?

"You okay?" Cabe asked. Alana hadn't even heard him enter the trailer.

"Fine." She wiped her eyes. "My headache's making my eyes water."

Since when do you lie to Cabe?

He sat down on the bench seat opposite her, his long legs stretched out in front of him.

"How long were you and Trent sleeping together?"

He knew. She shouldn't be surprised that he'd figured it out. She could tell he knew she'd been crying, too.

"Long enough."

Beneath his black hat, Cabe's eyes danced around her face, scanning the depths of her eyes. "Do you love him?"

She stood at the edge of the cliff. Then jumped.

"Yes."

"Then why are you in here crying? And why is Trent on his way back home?"

So he was gone.

"It would have never worked." She wiped her eyes again. "He's a rodeo—" she searched for the right word "—legend.

I'm not the type of woman that could ever hold his interest for long."

And where had that *come from?*

"Give me a break."

"Not to mention he lives in Colorado."

"So?"

She shook her head sharply. "I'm not leaving you guys, Cabe. You know what it's like with Rana. She needs me."

"She would survive."

"Yeah, but I would feel guilty as hell."

"Sounds like an excuse."

She inhaled sharply.

"If you love him, things will work out."

"Not without one of us having to give up a huge part of our lives."

"Sometimes love means sacrifice."

"One of us would end up resentful."

"Sounds like you're scared."

"I'm not scared."

"Yes, you are. Rana would be fine, Alana. Trust me. It's not like she doesn't have me to lean on."

"Cabe—"

"So don't use her as an excuse."

"I'm not."

"You're scared."

"No."

"You're afraid something else bad will happen if you leave the ranch."

"That's not it at all."

"What's more, you're making a huge mistake." He fingered the brim of his hat. "Trent's a good man. Sure, he might live in another state, and sure, you two might have to work out some sort of arrangement in order to see each other, but if you love him, that won't be a problem."

"I'm not scared."

Aren't you?

Okay, so maybe she was a little, but that was irrelevant.

"Then call Trent right now. Tell him to turn around. Tell him you were wrong."

She felt as if someone sat on her chest. She tried to inhale. Tried to simply breathe. "I can't," she said, tears filling her eyes again. "I just can't."

And instead of comforting her, Cabe just stared at her.

Rana came bounding in then, the girl's bright eyes losing their luster when she spotted the tears in Alana's eyes.

"What's wrong?" she asked.

"Nothing." Alana forced a smile. "Just a headache." That was true now. "I'm sorry I missed your performance, kiddo. How'd you do?"

"I did great!" Rana plopped next to her dad, her hat nearly knocked from her head she sat so down hard. "Scooter was sooooo perfect. I ended up second, but afterward Trent came over and gave me some more pointers. You should have seen it. Everyone gathered around. People were asking for his autograph. It was *so* embarrassing."

He'd stuck around. For Rana. Why did that make her feel like crying all over again?

"I told everyone to leave him alone," Rana was saying. "But he didn't seem to mind. Oh." She sat up straighter. "He gave me something to give you." She fished around in her pocket. "Here."

A letter. Her heart leaped into his chest.

"Come on," Cabe said. "Let's get Scooter loaded." He stood, motioning for Rana to follow.

Alana stared at the letter long after they left. Afraid. Hearing the sounds of the rodeo going on outside, yet not really hearing the applause from the crowd, the shouts of the cowboys, the moans of the cows.

Crap.

She unfolded the paper.

Alana—
I'm not giving up. I'm going to do what you said. I'm
going to make it to the NFR and I'll be thinking of you
the whole way. Afterward, I'm coming back for you. Win
or lose. I don't care. If I have to I'll quit competing. I'll
settle down in Colorado, or California. Wherever you are.
In the meantime I'll stay away. But only until after the
NFR. Then I'm coming for you. Perhaps by then you'll
get it through your fool head that what we have is real,
and that I love you.
Trent

She had tears running down her face, tears she hadn't even
noticed.
The letter fell from her grasp.

Chapter Twenty-Four

He rode like a man on fire.

It was big news in the rodeo world—how Trent Anderson overcame his horrific injuries and the death of his best friend, all so he could win another round at the NFR in Dustin's memory.

Alana told herself not to watch him on TV. It was too painful. Yet she couldn't seem to stop herself. He stuck with team roping, Mac his constant partner. After a month he sat thirty-first in the nation. After two months he sat twentieth. By the beginning of October, he'd almost cracked the top fifteen.

And the flowers... Roses. Daisies. Mums. Always something. And somehow, crazily, instead of fading, her love for him only grew.

"Did you see!" Rana cried, bursting into her apartment without so much as a knock. "He did it, Alana! Trent qualified."

She held a sheet of paper in her hand, a printout, Alana realized, of the top leaders in the country. Trent's name sat at number twelve.

"He did it!" Rana said again.

Yes, he had, Alana thought, the paper she held suddenly trembling thanks to her shaky hands.

"Are we going to Las Vegas to watch? It's only an eight-hour drive. I know. I looked it up."

Go to the NFR? To watch Trent?

"Why would we do that?"

"Because you've been moping around here for months," Rana said sternly. "I'm not an idiot, Aunt Alana. You fell in love with him, didn't you?"

"Rana—"

"You did, didn't you? My dad and I talked about it the other day. He said you're afraid to leave the ranch, afraid to leave *me*."

He'd told her that?

"Rana, that's not true." Not really.

"Isn't it?"

She couldn't look the girl in the eye.

Rana bent down close to her, forcing her to meet her gaze. "Aunt Alana," she said softly, firmly. "I'd rather suffer through a million nightmares alone than watch you be unhappy."

"Oh, Rana."

She realized in that instant that Rana wasn't a little girl anymore. Somehow, without Alana noticing, she'd turned into a young lady, her eyes more wise than she'd ever seen them before.

"You love him, Aunt Alana. Don't bother to deny it because I can see it in your eyes. What's more, you're going to go see him."

ONE MORE DAY, Trent thought. One more day and the waiting would be over. The hard work. The long weekends. The miles and miles of road traveled—all culminating in his first ride at the NFR.

"You nervous, buddy?" Mac asked, clapping him on the back.

They'd just finished practicing in the Thomas & Mack Center, the two of them keeping their horses in the portable stalls set up on the grounds just for contestant horses, which meant they were outside, and it was cold. Trent was thinking he would need to blanket Dee tonight. Poor horse would freeze to death otherwise.

"Not nervous. Just anxious."

Steam rose off Dee's brown-and-white back where the saddle had sat. Trent wondered if he should put a blanket on the horse now. The last thing Dee needed was a sore back.

"You still gonna quit afterward?"

He dropped his horse's bridle, slipping the halter on right after, and his horse tried to rub an itchy spot on his head on Trent's arm.

"Stop that," he ordered.

"Well, are you?" Mac persisted, his own horse already unsaddled, too.

"You don't have to."

He jerked upright in shock because he recognized that voice. *Alana*.

"I've lived five months without you. I think I can handle the weekends."

He caught Mac's eyes. The shock on his face was all the confirmation Trent needed.

"And I'm so sorry I kept us apart for even that long."

Slowly, he faced her, a part of him irrationally afraid that he might somehow scare Alana off if he turned too quickly.

She had tears in her eyes.

"I think…" He saw her lips tremble. "I think I needed the time apart. Think I needed to get my head sorted out."

"I know." He swallowed, realized his own throat was thick with tears. "Cabe told me what was going on."

The words didn't seem to surprise her. If anything, her smile grew.

"I was afraid." She dropped her gaze for a moment before lifting it again. "I just couldn't believe that this could be real. That I could have fallen in love so quickly, so completely."

"Alana—"

He opened his arms.

She sank into them, and Trent closed his eyes and inhaled her scent and thought he didn't give a rat's ass if he never won the NFR again—as long as she was in his arms.

"I love you."

A tear hit his cheek leaving a hot streak behind. "I know."

"But even though Rana's okay with it, I really don't want to abandon her altogether."

He held her even tighter. "I know. That's why Cabe and I worked out a schedule. We'll spend our summers in California, winters in Colorado. There's plenty of rodeos on the West Coast to keep me busy."

It must have been the right thing to say, because suddenly she buried her head in his arms. He rested his head on her hair, held her, catching Mac's own teary-eyed gaze as he walked by, leaving them alone with nothing but the horses, a breeze and Nevada's silver sky.

"You have to promise me something, Trent Anderson," she said a long while later.

"Anything."

She drew back, stared into his eyes. "You better win the average—for Dustin...and Braden...and Kim."

"I will."

She lifted a hand to his cheek. "I love you."

He smiled. "I know."

And two weeks later, he did exactly as promised—he won the average at the National Finals Rodeo, but it was nothing compared to winning Alana's heart.

* * * * *

Be sure to look for Pamela Britton's next American Romance book in November 2013!

REQUEST YOUR FREE BOOKS!
2 FREE NOVELS PLUS 2 FREE GIFTS!

HARLEQUIN®

American ★ Romance®

LOVE, HOME & HAPPINESS

YES! Please send me 2 FREE Harlequin® American Romance® novels and my 2 FREE gifts (gifts are worth about $10). After receiving them, if I don't wish to receive any more books, I can return the shipping statement marked "cancel." If I don't cancel, I will receive 4 brand-new novels every month and be billed just $4.74 per book in the U.S. or $5.24 per book in Canada. That's a savings of at least 14% off the cover price! It's quite a bargain! Shipping and handling is just 50¢ per book in the U.S. and 75¢ per book in Canada.* I understand that accepting the 2 free books and gifts places me under no obligation to buy anything. I can always return a shipment and cancel at any time. Even if I never buy another book, the two free books and gifts are mine to keep forever.

154/354 HDN F4YN

Name _____ (PLEASE PRINT)

Address _____ Apt. #

City _____ State/Prov. _____ Zip/Postal Code

Signature (if under 18, a parent or guardian must sign)

Mail to the **Harlequin® Reader Service:**
IN U.S.A.: P.O. Box 1867, Buffalo, NY 14240-1867
IN CANADA: P.O. Box 609, Fort Erie, Ontario L2A 5X3

Want to try two free books from another line?
Call 1-800-873-8635 or visit www.ReaderService.com.

* Terms and prices subject to change without notice. Prices do not include applicable taxes. Sales tax applicable in N.Y. Canadian residents will be charged applicable taxes. Offer not valid in Quebec. This offer is limited to one order per household. Not valid for current subscribers to Harlequin American Romance books. All orders subject to credit approval. Credit or debit balances in a customer's account(s) may be offset by any other outstanding balance owed by or to the customer. Please allow 4 to 6 weeks for delivery. Offer available while quantities last.

Your Privacy—The Harlequin® Reader Service is committed to protecting your privacy. Our Privacy Policy is available online at www.ReaderService.com or upon request from the Harlequin Reader Service.

We make a portion of our mailing list available to reputable third parties that offer products we believe may interest you. If you prefer that we not exchange your name with third parties, or if you wish to clarify or modify your communication preferences, please visit us at www.ReaderService.com/consumerschoice or write to us at Harlequin Reader Service Preference Service, P.O. Box 9062, Buffalo, NY 14269. Include your complete name and address.

HAR13R

THE RANCHER'S HOMECOMING

by Cathy McDavid

Annie Hennessee has her hands full with rebuilding the Sweetheart Inn following a devastating forest fire. But what is Sam Wyler doing back in town? Isn't it enough that he broke Annie's heart all those years ago?

A figure emerged from the shadows. A man. He wore jeans and boots, and a black cowboy hat was pulled low over his brow.

Even so, she instantly recognized him, and her broken heart beat as if it was brand-new.

Sam! He was back. After nine years.

Why? And what was he doing at the Gold Nugget?

"Annie?" He started down the stairs, the confused expression on his face changing to one of recognition. "It's you!"

Suddenly nervous, she retreated. If he hadn't seen her, she'd have run.

No, that was a stupid reaction. She wasn't young and vulnerable anymore. She was thirty-four. The mother of a three-year-old child. Grown. Confident. Strong.

And yet the door beckoned. He'd always had that effect on her, been able to strip away her defenses.

A rush of irritation, more at herself than him, galvanized her.

"What are you doing here?"

Ignoring her question, he descended the stairs, his boots making contact with the wooden steps one at a time. Lord, it seemed to take forever.

This wasn't, she recalled, the first time he'd kept her waiting. Or the longest.

At last he stood before her, tall, handsome and every inch the rugged cowboy she remembered.

"Hey, girl, how are you? I wasn't sure you still lived in Sweetheart."

He spoke with an ease that gave no hint of those last angry words they'd exchanged, and he even used his once-familiar endearment for her. He might have swept her into a hug if Annie hadn't stepped to the side.

"Still here."

"I heard about the inn." Regret filled his voice. "I'm sorry."

"Me, too." She lifted her chin. "We're going to rebuild. As soon as we settle with the insurance company."

"You look good." His gaze never left her face. She was grateful he didn't seem to notice her khaki uniform, rumpled and soiled after a day in the field. Or her hair escaping her ponytail and hanging in limp tendrils. Her lack of makeup.

"Th-thank you."

"Been a while."

"Quite a while."

His blue eyes transfixed her, as they always had, and she felt her bones melt.

Dammit! Her entire world had fallen apart the past six weeks. She didn't need Sam showing up, kicking at the pieces.

Will Sam turn out to be a help or a hindrance to Annie's attempts to rebuild her life?

Find out in THE RANCHER'S HOMECOMING by Cathy McDavid, book one of her new SWEETHEART, NEVADA trilogy.

Available in July 2013, only from Harlequin American Romance.